tly until, in
sense
danger, turn, ... outh hideous,
his roar thundering, his stroke ferocious and
lightning swift. By then, it is too late . . .

But now he senses danger. *They* are coming after *him* . . . closing in. The silence of the forest is disturbed. Grizzly is not afraid. Unsuspected by his pursuers, he has a plan!

Grizzly

Will Collins

CORONET BOOKS
Hodder and Stoughton

First published 1976 by Pyramid Books Inc., New York

Coronet Edition 1976

The characters and situations in this book are entirely imaginary and bear no relation to any real person or actual happening

Printed and bound in Great Britain for
Coronet Books, Hodder and Stoughton, London,
by Hazell Watson & Viney Ltd,
Aylesbury, Bucks

ISBN 0 340 21551 8

PROLOGUE

The beast had been on the move for more than a week. Always alert to subtle changes in the sounds and movement around him, he had altered his territorial roamings in an attempt to avoid the noisy, foul-smelling machines that had appeared some months ago.

Although the beast did not think as humans do, or measure time in days and weeks and months, he had an inborn sense of the passage of the phases of the moon and the climatic shiftings of wind and rain and snow. He had holed up for the winter months, when the blizzards howled through the high country, and when he emerged it should have been to an orgy of eating and lazy days of warm sun.

Instead, he found angry steel machinery chewing away at the base of his mountain. The beast knew nothing of oil shale, and he had spent his entire life avoiding the two-legged enemy, Man. The smell of the invader offended his keen nose, and the stench of the gasoline exhaust and diesel fumes fouled the air for miles around the shale excavations.

At first, he moved back into the recesses of the high country. But, relentlessly, the men and their machines followed.

The beast had always been alone. From his birth, six winters ago, he had been shunned by his own kind and driven away by females who should have been eager for mating. His instincts fought with his awareness that he was somehow different, but he eventually accepted his role as outsider, and marked out his territory with claw marks and droppings, and defended it against all intruders.

But the two-legged ones came in great numbers, and their machines tore away at his trails and the trees he had marked so carefully. He would have fought, but something in the back of his mind warned him against that.

So, as they followed him up the invisibly rich outcroppings of oil-saturated shale, the beast was slowly, but inevitably driven away from his hunting grounds.

There was nothing to do but accept it. He would find food somewhere else.

CHAPTER ONE

The entrance to the National Park was mostly parking area. In recent years, day visitors had been urged not to drive into the park, with free trams offered instead to transport them from scenic point to point. The narrow blacktop roads had been turning into fume-choked parking lots. Now, trams running every fifteen minutes, most cars remained outside the park in the huge lots that were patrolled by rangers who protected the vehicles against pilferage and theft.

Near the park land, but not on it, were private vendors selling gifts, food, cocktails. The Park Service frowned on such activity, but there was little that could be done about it. A private individual on his own land had a right to go into business. And, because of recent attacks on the zoning system caused by the attempt to provide suburban housing for minorities, the Park Service was wary of trying to invoke local zoning to chase away the junky businesses that often gathered near the park gates.

Besides, the tourists *wanted* to buy the junk. They grabbed for the little carved bears, with their cute noses painted black. That was something to show back home, a souvenir of their visit to the high country. Clay pottery, decorated with zig-zagged Indian patterns, dangled from colored hemp ropes—indoor planters supposedly created by the displaced tribes who had once roamed these mountains. Actually, they were mass-produced in Mexico.

Since the gasoline shortage had become acute, the Park Service had gradually shifted its preference in vehicles toward the foreign, four-cylinder off-road copies of the Land Rover. One of these approached the gate now. It was painted a deep green, with the Service's new sky, water and land emblem painted on its side. The vehicle was made by Toyota.

The same emblem was splashed across the big sign that read, 'WELCOME TO YOUR NATIONAL PARK.'

The ranger vehicle moved past a long line of cars and pickup trucks with campers mounted in their beds. The occupants were a cross section of the population. Some were very young, with long hair and hopeful beards. Some were senior citizens, bald or grey-haired. And most were families, with two or three children. An occasional expensive RV, a self-contained house on wheels, waited democratically in the line of poorer visitors.

Inside the gate, and down the road toward the lake, the ranger vehicle passed the new arrivals who were setting up their camp sites.

Some had surplus pup tents. These were the younger contingent, usually traveling in an old VW beetle or on a pair of Honda trail bikes.

Others had nylon umbrella tents, bought this spring from Sears, or Montgomery Ward. These older, more experienced campers, had brought folding chairs and tables, and bright green Coleman lanterns.

The elite were the motorhomes, parked in the full sites with electrical supply and water hookups.

A red Dodge van has just pulled up to a vacant spot, and the driver was starting to unload a tent, while his wife and small boy set up a folding table.

The ranger vehicle stopped.

The ranger leaned out.

The ranger was a slim girl, tightly contained in a uniform that seemed a size too small.

She said, to the man wrestling with the canvas tent, 'Hi, mister.'

He looked up. 'Hi.'

She pointed at the windshield of the van. 'You don't have a sticker for your camp site.'

Puzzled, he said, 'Do we need one?'

'You sure do. Or they'll assign it to somebody else and you'll have to leave.'

'I didn't know. What should we do?'

'Leave your stuff here to hold the site. Drive back to the gate and tell them where you are. This is N-43.'

'Hey,' he said. 'That's real nice of you.'

'No sweat,' she said. 'Tell them Gail sent you.'

The man grinned. 'Gail the ranger?'

'That's me,' said the girl. She gave a casual wave and drove on down the road. She checked in the mirror, however, and smiled when she saw the man closing the rear door of the van and getting in, starting to drive back up the road to the gate.

He'd been lucky. By four in the afternoon, most locations would be gone, and he would have had to find a motel out on the private land, or head over to the nearest town, High City, more than a mile away.

Gail turned the green vehicle onto a rutted dirt road, and almost instantly caught a glimpse of a speckled fawn, lying under a spruce tree. The doe would be around somewhere nearby.

Yes, there on the skyline.

The deer's ears flicked up. But the animal recognized the sound of the vehicle as a friendly one, and there was no fear shown.

This was the long way to the ranger station, but it was Gail's favorite, because few of the visitors ever drove along it and the wild life had adopted it as a private enclave.

In the trees were deer, and the occasional shy black bear, and many partridges. By the dirt shoulder were often quail and aggressive skunks, meandering along as if they owned the mountain . . . which, in fact, they did as far as Gail was concerned. In the stream, which paralleled the road for a few hundred yards, an energetic family of beaver were trying to erect a dam of cut saplings. The rangers disapproved, because the water was needed further down the mountain, but so far no one had volunteered to destroy the half-finished blockade.

Gail Nelson was a city girl, raised and educated in Cleveland. She had come to the western wilderness as a tourist, fell in love with it, and abandoned her college education to train as a ranger. She still got letters from her mother filled with subtle hints that Harry Bennedict, the second assistant vice president at the Gates Mills bank was still single and lonely. Gail responded with friendly gossip about the animals she had befriended, and Polaroid photos of her with her favorite horse, Tex, who had been named after the popular western singer, Tex Ritter. Ritter's recording of the title song of the film 'High Noon' was on he juke box at the settlement restaurant, and was nearly worn out by the dimes and quarters Gail's fellow rangers fed into it, because they knew how much the song pleased her.

Gail's foot stabbed at the brake, and the vehicle made ruts in the rocky dirt road as it skidded to a stop.

She smiled and gave a toot on the horn.

The matronly opossum, a plump, grey-haired marsupial with three baby possums hanging from her upraised, hairless tail, continued across the road without even looking around.

'You show 'em, mama,' said Gail Nelson.

These were the good days, after the season was over, and the influx of visitors dwindled to just a few hundred a day. There would be fewer lost children to find; fewer drunks to quiet down.

And, she thought sourly, fewer drugstore cowboys to make snide passes at her when she came by their campsites, checking out unsafe fires and making sure they carried out all the tin cans they'd brought in.

Still, she told herself, she was apparently a growing girl yet, and it was time she spent the hundred and eleven dollars it would cost her to buy a larger uniform.

Next spring, she compromised. She didn't like grasping hands, but it was nice to have those admiring glances.

The road was clear now. She pressed the gas pedal and moved out.

The beast was finally forced over the divide between the valley where the oil shale mining was taking place, and into another forest, an unfamiliar one, where he had never been.

At the highest point, he had been nearly thirteen thousand feet up, and the bitter cold had not treated him well. He had tried to bite ice off an outcropping of rock, since there was no liquid water to be found, and a blinding pain had shot through his head, jabbing inside his skull. He leaped back, but it was too late; one of his incisors had broken off almost even with the gum line, and as it began to throb with a steady pulse, the beast raised his head and gave a low wail of pain that increased until a nearby tern flushed and flew away, its wings making a fluttering, beating sound that only increased the beast's anger and frustration.

CHAPTER TWO

Rangers are inclined to be solitary people.

Until recently, their ranks were filled only with men. Even the Susan B. Anthonys of the world, seeking equality in a male-oriented society had little taste for the deep woods and the High Sierras.

But after the Second World War, a new breed of young woman began to emerge. Akin to her pioneer grandmother, she sought adventure on skis and with climbing cramp-ons on treacherous mountain peaks. And she discovered the wonder of the wild life that shared the forests alongside man-made roads and settlements, often unobserved by anyone except the most persistent and gentle viewer.

One cannot crash through a forest with a transistor radio blaring in the calm, still air, and expect to see anything except a distant, flying hawk. One cannot blunder through the trees, crushing dry deadfalls underfoot, and expect to hear anything except a chipmunk diving for cover under a pile of brush. One cannot harness mechanical horsepower and roar through the woods on a trail bike and expect to find anything except frightened tracks showing where the wild life has fled the noisy trails.

On foot is the best way to explore the woods. The Indian found his game food because he respected its sense of privacy; instead of changing his environment, the Indian adapted to it and so survived.

But the white man, accustomed to 'taming' the wilderness only succeeded in destroying much of it. And many of his worst depravations have been committed in the name of preserving the wild.

Gail Nelson hoped to be part of the new breed of forest ranger who would help turn the trend around. This was only her second year with the Service, but she had already made a mark with her superiors, who saw in her a hope for the future.

Even in this post-season period, there wasn't time to roam the woods on foot. So today, as usual, Gail would saddle up Tex and set off on her rounds, her healthy young body straining the seams of the uniform she admitted she really *must* replace by next season.

The ranger station was constructed of split pine, and fitted into the clearing which surrounded it like a piece of the forest circled by a lake of gravel and asphalt.

Outside the building, a group of rangers were lined up, standing at ease. Their brown and green uniforms were trim and neat, however, and their attention on the ranger who stood before them was keen.

He looked up as Gail Nelson parked her vehicle. Without making it a big thing, he glanced at his watch, and she saw the glance. She gave a little, 'I couldn't help it,' movement of her hand and head, and he smiled, motioning her into the line of rangers.

All of the others were men; most of them were in their late twenties, although a few were younger.

'I didn't think you'd make it,' said the ranger who stood alone.

Gail said, 'I wouldn't miss a Kelly Gordon briefing for the world.'

This sent a chuckling series of remarks down the line of rangers. They were friendly gibes, most of them, about how women were always late.

'I had to straighten out a camper at the "N" site,' Gail said without apology.

Kelly nodded. 'You're late, but we're just starting.'

Tom Cooper, a young ranger, slipped down the line so he could stand next to Gail. She gave him a half smile, trying to keep the side of her lips that faced toward Kelly Gordon, immobile.

Kelly said, 'We've got us a problem and a half today. This is the biggest post-season mob we've ever had. If we're not careful, they can get out of hand.'

Tom Cooper said, maybe a bit too loudly, 'Kelly's worried that we've got more back-packers up there in the high country than raccoons.'

Gail winced. Tom was too obviously trying to draw attention to himself while poking fun, not too subtly, at his supervisor. She had warned him more than once about this. But he didn't seem to be able to control his mouth.

Kelly ignored the remark. 'So I'm sending patrols out to Area Four,' he went on. 'No way of knowing what might happen. The long-range weather's good, but we could get a freak storm, or a fire or anything.'

Gail, to keep Tom from mouthing off again, said, 'There's no way to wet-nurse all those back-packers. There's too many of them scattered too far.'

'I know,' said Kelly. 'But we'll still do the best we can.' He looked down the line of rangers. 'Okay, you've all got your jobs. Go do them.'

The casual line broke up. The teams of rangers moved off toward their vehicles or the stable.

Kelly waited, as Gail Nelson came toward him. He wanted to smile at her anxiety, at her fresh young face and ripe figure bulging through her underestimated uniform. He had made up his mind to mention its tightness to her if she didn't do something by next season; there was so little time to go this year, it wasn't worth the hassle. Privately, he believed that she wouldn't need prompting. She had a good head.

At thirty-eight, Kelly looked five years younger. His dark blue eyes and sleek brown hair gave him the appearance of an actor. In fact, once while in New York, he had been offered the starring role in a shaving cream commercial. He had turned it down when he learned he was expected to wear makeup. Often, Kelly had wondered what might have happened to his life if he had taken the job.

Kelly was born in Montana, and grew up in the snow country. His friends often said (out of his hearing) that Kelly was suckled by a bear and raised by a bobcat. Actually, his parents were normal folks in Helena, but there was a great deal of emphasis on hunting and fishing, and Kelly excelled at both of them.

He brought down his first twelve-point deer before his fifteenth birthday, and for several years after that, kept the Gordon freezer filled with game.

Then, one day, he had seen his best friend shot down by a city hunter who made a sound shot into the brush with a high-powered thirty-ought-six rifle. The slug was an expanding soft-point, and after it tore through the unlucky young man, there was never a chance of saving his life. Kelly had shoved handfuls of his shirt into the wound, and never even slowed the bleeding.

Since that day, he had never shot at a living thing.

When he was drafted for the Vietnam war, he did not refuse to go. Instead, he explained his feelings to the officials, and volunteered for the most dangerous medic duty available. Several times, he'd flown with Don Stober, four years his junior. But he trusted Don, and when Stober had shown up after the war, looking for a job, Kelly had interceded for him and helped him get the flying ranger post.

Kelly liked Gail Nelson. She wasn't the first female ranger who had served at his park. But she was the most popular one. She had a serious dedication to the work, and a real love of the wilderness and its animals.

She told him, 'I'm sorry. My apologies.'

'Accepted,' he said, with his best Charlton Heston grimness. It fooled nobody.

Tom said, apparently to Kelly, but actually to Gail, 'Well, I'm on my way up to R-Four.'

She said, 'That's pretty crowded. Maybe the two of us should go?'

And this was as much to Kelly as to Tom.

The idea of Gail joining him appealed to Tom Cooper. To Kelly, eagerly, he said, 'R-Four is loaded, Kell. And a lot of those back-packers up there are green as grass.'

Kelly looked at the work sheet on his clip board and shook his head.

'Gail, I need you down here today. Thompson phoned in sick, so the home base is all yours.'

She nodded, flashing a smile that she hoped would hide her disappointment. 'Good,' she said. 'Maybe I can get my paperwork up to date.'

Tom shrugged. Moving toward his jeep, one of the last of the old American vehicles left in the park, he told Gail, in a low voice that Kelly couldn't hear, 'Well, we tried. Listen, I'll catch you later for dinner.'

She nodded, warming up the smile especially for him. Tom raised his voice and said, confident that Kelly would overhear, 'See you later.'

Automatically, Gail replied, 'Alligator.'

'Hey,' Kelly called. 'You can't get up to R-Four in that four-wheeler.'

Caught in mid-stride, Tom halted, grinned. 'How true,' he said. 'I don't know what I was thinking of.'

Gail looked away. She concealed the laugh that tried to burst forth. Tom Cooper's activities in the back of a jeep were the talk of the younger rangers. And one *could* reach R-Four by jeep, if the driver was willing to risk a bashed-in oil pan while climbing a steep, rock-filled grade near the regular trail.

'Take Tex,' Gail said. 'He needs the exercise.'

'Thanks,' Tom said. He sauntered off toward the stable.

Two other rangers, giving their Toyota imitation Land Rover a walk-around check, had observed the brief scene.

'Tom's pissed,' said one.

'Naw,' said the other. 'He knows Kelly's got eyes for that chick with all the cameras. Gail's as safe down here as she'd be back in Cleveland.'

Dryly, the other ranger said, 'And exactly how safe is that?'

The beast did not like this side of the mountain. It was quiet enough, but the scent of the two-legged enemy was everywhere.

The pain in his jaw was unrelenting. It throbbed with

every movement, and as he breathed, the cold air seared the exposed nerve ends with an agony that was almost unbearable. It was this more than hunger and thirst that forced him down toward the valley, where the air was warmer and the pain less intense.

Almost as intense was his hunger. The pain from the fractured tooth seemed to affect his sight, and more importantly, his keen sense of smell. Twice now, he had come up on edible game and lost that first, unexpected, move because of his diminished senses. Both animals—one a small deer, the other a scraggly goat—got away with frightened leaps.

Although the beast could run faster than a man, and almost as fast as a horse, he stumbled on the icy slopes, and watched, in pain-shattered anger, as his food-to-be escaped down the mountain.

High country back-pack area R-Four was located just below the timber line, where tall pines and spruces suddenly leaped from the steep incline. No lumberjack's axe had ever touched so much as a twig of these trees, and some of them were older than the nation whose banner flew from the ranger station's flagpole. Pine cones as large as a baby's head scattered over the forest floor, and when the conditions of sun and moisture and soil were right, another tree would germinate and begin to grow.

But in the forest interior there is never much sunlight. At noon, perhaps, a single ray will penetrate the thick trees and touch the dark pine-needle-strewn earth for a few moments, then move on, racing up the sides of the mountain as if trying to paint it all golden before the onset of night.

To some, the interior of the forest is cathedral-like. It is an obvious comparison. The shafts of golden light, beaming down through majestic giants whose growth rings traced time back to the time of Christ.

A skilled woodsman will see one thing as he moves through the forest; an amateur, however well-read in forest lore, will see another. To him will come a sense of apprehension, of disassociation. It is very easy to become foolishly lost in the forest, and when the beginner does so, panic is his neighbor. This feeling of tingly near-fear is one of the attractions that brings so many to the woods today. True danger is never really present, but it *might* be, and that is its allure.

The woodsman has learned not to laugh at the tenderfoot. Because at least the beginner is trying to learn. Too many today cannot be bothered, too many see the wilderness as a resource to be harvested.

Careful harvesting is not only possible, it is desirable, for the wilderness can go mad in its prolific growth, just as the population explosion has jammed the globe with too many breathing, eating, polluting humans. Thinning out is necessary. But it must be done with care, and with love. Neither commodity is ever present when human greed directs the work.

But this forest was protected. Against everything except its own mavericks.

June Hamilton and Margaret Rogers were almost twins, in birth dates at least. June was born on August 11th, and Margaret on the 12th. Both had attended Penn State, although only June was from Pennsylvania—Lancaster, where the Pennsylvania Dutch still plod along the highways in their horse-drawn black carriages. Margaret was from Elizabethtown, Kentucky, and had gone to Penn on a scholarship.

Both girls had been trapped in a liberal arts program, but in their last year had tried to remedy that disastrous choice by electing a new major, Ecology Management. With the growth of environmental protection, whole new industries had sprung up to provide the air scrubbers for smoke stacks, the filters and processors for waste dispersal, the test equipment to detect violations in air and water pollution. So rapidly did the new industry grow that it, in itself, became guilty of the very violations it had formed to correct.

New ideas were needed. So young people in college moved toward this latest frontier.

It had been Margaret's idea to come out here to the park

and camp for a week. She argued, 'We're city people. We've been trained to restore the environment back to its natural state. But what, actually, do we know about it? Only what we've read in the Sierra Club books.'

They'd spent most of the summer planning the trip and buying the equipment and gear needed.

Now, the vacation—or 'field trip,' as Margaret preferred to call it, was almost over.

The girls had been exploring one side of the mountain. They had awakened at dawn, as always. It's hard to sleep late in the woods. Too much life begins to move around you.

No photograph or motion picture can ever capture the incredible shocking beauty of mountain peaks, looming over the visitor to the high country.

Their summits, tipped with silver, seem to hang in the sky. It is as if they are falling at you through the crisp clear air.

And the silence is immense. A bird can be heard a mile away. The distant tinkle of water falling down the mountainside is as melodic as the gentle swirl of a Chopin piano sonata.

The girls, who had climbed almost to the nine-thousand-foot level, paused. They watched the clouds painting wispy shadows over the mountains for a while.

June said, then, 'Hey, we're not mountain climbers. Besides, this is our last day. We've got to get organized.'

'What's to organize?' asked Margaret, tossing her short blonde hair. 'We'll just throw everything in the packs and hike on down the mountain.'

'*With* our garbage,' June reminded. 'Remember? No more burning the tin cans and burying them. Those days are over. That ranger made a big point of our not turning this place into a land fill.'

'Relax,' said her friend. 'I've even been washing out the cans so they won't smell.'

Now, near their camp, they moved carefully through the darkly shadowed forest, and felt that sense of cool distance from civilization that always comes when one is surrounded by trees without a single sign of human existence in sight.

They had chosen, as their camp site, one of the few clearings that enjoyed more than an hour of sunlight a day. June had demanded it, once they discovered the clearing. She said, 'Do you know how long it would take to dry out a pair of undies under those pines?' and Margaret, sensibly, agreed—although she would have preferred to pitch camp further up the mountain.

Puffing as she climbed a rock fracture, June said, 'Hey, Maggie, what do we have to eat?'

'I put the rest of the stew in the Dutch oven,' said Margaret. 'I left it in the embers.'

'Embers?'

'I know you're not supposed to, but we've got rocks all around the fire, and it's right out in the middle of the clearing. What could happen?'

June's hair, longer than Maggie's, and a dark red, caught in the pitch-choked branch of one of the young pines. She yanked it free with a very unlady-like swear-word.

A moment later, they stepped into their clearing, and Maggie let out a little yip of fright.

Tom Cooper, astride Tex, looked down at the girls with a half-smile.

'Is this your camp?' he asked.

'Yes,' said June, hesitantly. 'You gave us a shock.'

'Sorry. Hi there.'

June said, 'Hi.'

Maggie, not as friendly, said, 'Thanks for scaring us.'

'I said I was sorry. But you were bad girls. You left a fire smouldering.'

'We were cooking,' Maggie said defensively.

'No excuse. Not when there's nobody present. Do you know how fast a fire could go through these trees?'

June said, chagrined, 'We know. It was stupid.'

'I guess you've got a camping permit?'

Still hostile, Maggie said, 'Do you want to see it?'

Tom shook his head. 'No, I believe you. But do me a favor?'

June said, 'What?'

'Watch yourselves up here. Stay out of trouble.'

'What kind of trouble?'

He shrugged. 'Nothing special. Just don't take unnecessary risks. This high country is treacherous. You could take a fall, sprain an ankle. Anything. And it's easy to get turned around, lose your bearings.'

Maggie said, 'Believe me, Ranger, we aren't about to get ourselves lost.'

'Okay,' he said. 'When are you coming down?'

June said, 'This afternoon. After we eat, and clean up the area.'

He nodded. 'I'll watch for you.'

June offered, 'How about hanging around for a few minutes? Maggie makes a great stew.'

Not really tempted, Tom shook his head. 'Thanks, but no. I've got a heavy dinner date tonight. Just don't forget to check out at the ranger station before you leave the park. We like to know that all of our campers are down safe. And it saves a lot of search parties getting frozen looking for somebody who didn't check out and went back to Iowa while we were trying to rescue them where they weren't.'

Coldly, Maggie said, 'We aren't children, Ranger.'

He looked at her full figure under the bright yellow blouse and grinned.

'No, ma'am,' he said. 'You sure aren't.'

June said, 'Don't worry. We'll be down before dark.'

'Fine,' said Tom. 'I'll probably see you then.'

He touched the brim of his hat with a finger and rode down the trail.

June watched after him. 'Not bad,' she said.

Maggie sniffed. 'If you like the type.'

June smiled. 'I like the type.'

Hunger had replaced pain as the chief concern of the beast. It had been more than a full day since he had eaten.

In winter, he was able to curl up and subsist off the stored energy of his fat. But when on the move, as he was now, he needed huge quantities of food. Far more than the others of his species, for the beast knew that he was much larger than his cousins on the mountain.

But game was scarce on this side of the divide. He had trouble smelling the spoor, with the pain shooting up through his head from the shattered tooth, and his eyesight was so poor that he was virtually dependent on his nose as his best method of detecting food.

Halfway down the steep slopes, he stopped, lifted his head and sniffed.

Even with the pain, he knew what that scent was.

Fresh blood.

Food.

CHAPTER THREE

The blood spoor was closer. The beast moved through the forest, sniffing at the rotted leaves, until he came to a stream.

He explored it with his nose, hesitated.

Yes. The scent came from upstream.

Slowly, he began to climb the slope along the edge of the stream's rushing water.

'Illegal or not,' said June Hamilton, 'this is one damned good stew.'

'I thank you,' said Maggie Rogers. 'Too bad your sexy ranger friend didn't stay around to share it.'

'Oh, lay off,' said June. 'I thought he was nice.'

'So nice you did everything but zip down your jeans for him.'

'No way,' said June. 'Not this time of month.'

'Well, how about that? Saved by nature and the eternal curse.'

'There's always next week,' said June, fluffing her dark red hair.

Disgusted, Maggie said, 'Is that all you think of? Sex?'

'Ho, ho,' said June. 'Am I really hearing this from the blonde who took on three, count 'em, three, members of the football team after the New Year's party?'

Maggie threw the remains of her meal into the fire. 'That's a stupid lie. I got a little drunk, and we necked, and that's all there was to it.'

'Not according to Matty Poole.'

'Matthew Poole is a compulsive liar, and his mind was marinated in the gutter. Listen, let's pack up and get out of here. It'll be dark early.'

June finished her stew. 'Okay,' she said. 'And for a would-be house mother, you still make a mighty fine stew.'

Maggie laughed. 'Many thanks,' she said. 'Now, let's stop

knifing each other like this. We both need all the help we can get.'

'Agreed,' said June. 'I'm sorry, babe.'

'Me too,' said Maggie. 'Hey, I'll get the fire, and you start on the tent.'

'In a minute,' said June. 'I've got to pee first.'

Maggie put a growl into her voice. 'Every time we have to take the tent down, it seems like you have to go pee.'

'Pavlov's reaction,' said June. 'I'll be right back.'

June giggled, and was gone into the deep recesses of the forest.

The beast lifted his nose and sniffed.

The blood spoor was so close now that he could almost feel its source within his claws. He gave a low growl.

Hunger fought with the pain in his jaw. Hunger won. He moved silently through the woods.

Maggie Rogers finished scattering the fire's ashes, and poured the last of the dish water over them. She put the remaining plastic forks into the garbage bag that they'd pack out with them. Plastic, it had turned out, endured forever, longer than metal, and leaving it lying around in the woods was almost as bad as running around starting forest fires.

She glanced at the pup tent, shook her head.

That was June's job, and she intended to leave it for the slim red-head.

She started to cram gear into the green back-pack.

Behind her, she heard a twig snap.

'Okay, June,' she said, not looking around. 'Get to work. Start on the tent. When I get through with these packs, I'll help you.'

There was no answer.

She turned, and saw the beast.

Only a slow motion camera could have recorded what happened in the next few seconds.

First, Maggie screamed.

But the sound had barely emerged from her strained throat when a huge paw, claws extended, whipped toward and *through* her. Incredulously, Maggie saw her arm sever itself from her body and fly through the air.

Her scream intensified. But it was not a scream of pain. The nerve shock was so intense that it had not yet been converted into pain.

She screamed with horror. She wanted to cry, *This can't be happening to me!* but instead all that came out of her contorted lips were little bleating sounds that overlapped words with mumbling sounds which, in another context, might have sounded like cries of passion.

'No, oh no, no, no, uh, no, no—'

The words had no effect on the beast. The blood spoor had led him to this place, and while he did not smell it on this creature, this living food, a new blood scent now filled his nostrils and he felt the lust of killing on him.

None of us are prepared for the assault that Margaret Rogers went through in those few seconds.

Natural death is kindly; it dulls the senses with toxic venoms that dull the mind and makes death actually welcome, so gentle and soft is its slowly-covering blanket.

But Maggie knew only terror and disbelief. Her blood was pulsing from her torn arm socket in six-foot jets, her organs had gone into final spasm, yet her mind was still alert and able to form sensible words.

'I'm dead!' she screamed. 'I'm dead! Leave me alone! Please! Please.'

The beast did not understand.

With a single stroke her chest was ripped open to and through the bones. What had been desirable breasts, cradled in lace only moments before now became raw, bleeding meat.

Maggie screamed once more. But now the assault on her body had progressed so far that her brain was blocked off from its life fluids, and with a final wail that only she heard, deep inside her mind, she watched the light of the world flicker out forever and the last word that choked from her bleeding lips was, 'Mommy!'

More than a hundred years ago, it had become apparent that unless wilderness areas were protected from the encroachment of man, they would vanish forever. Hunters, lumbermen, settlers and cattlemen were carving marks in the landscape that would never be restored to its original wild state. It took years of bitter dispute, as the interests of exploitation and conservation met in legislative battle. But eventually the National Park Service was formed, and the Department of the Interior began to acquire land that would be set aside for the benefit of unborn generations.

Ironically, the very protection the Park Service affords the environment sometimes results in its alteration. Only recently had the Service decided that perhaps it is best to let natural forest fires burn themselves out, even though that may produce a large area of ugly, blackened landscape. But nature intended such blights, and without them, the forest grows rampant, unchecked. Trees are choked by overgrowth, stunted, and the forest becomes an uncontrolled thicket.

Most of our sports have been corrupted into profitable industries, and back-packing is no exception. What was once a sensible way of traveling in the woods has been expanded into a giant catalogue of aluminum pack-frames, flame-orange duffle bags, freeze-dried rations, insulated hiking boots, two-way Citizen's Band radios, and Dacron windbreakers.

Yet the back-packers who hike into the interior of the national and state parks do find a sense of isolation and adventure that is denied to the thousands of other visitors who drive into the camp sites with their recreational vehicles, complete with air conditioning, television and flush toilets. When you're lying on your back in the new grass and glacier-flowers just above the 6,000-foot level, looking down at the fluffy clouds forming in the late morning, it's easy to imagine that you've been thrown back in time, back to an age without interstate highways and jet supersonic airplanes.

Then you look up, and see a National Park Service helicopter, its blades throbbing through the air with that eggbeater sound made so familiar by television coverage of the Vietnam war.

Donald Stober, piloting the Hughes 500 helicopter, did not consciously think of the impact the noisy machine was having on the forest below, but he was aware of it. By now the wild animals had become used to the noise, and being animals, they almost never looked up anyway. But the backpackers did, and some of them, angry at being dragged back to civilization by the ugly metal bird, made gestures toward it that weren't exactly friendly waves.

Don had flown two full tours of chopper service in South Vietnam, most of them on rescue and medical missions. Tall and slender, he looked more like a medical student than an experienced pilot and ranger.

Below the helicopter, the dark green of the forest blurred beneath its whirling blades.

Behind Don, in the passenger seat, two men sat. They were dressed in conservative business suits, totally useless in the wilderness below if the trusted chopper engine should ever shut down.

But it never had. And, Don thought, grinning, it probably never would. Which was too bad, because he would have enjoyed hiking out for several hours, followed by two sweating V.I.P.s wearing gray business suits and expensive alligator loafers.

Well, if he wanted to keep his flying time, this was a necessary payment of dues. Giving visiting firemen the grand tour.

His southern accent, created back in Cedartown, Georgia, was almost gone now; it had been more than six years since he had been home. At thirty-four, he sometimes lapsed into the 'good old boy' slang for fun, or for effect with a susceptible visitor from one of the cities that seemed to spew their two-week tourists at the parks with increasing numbers.

Don Stober's voice was slightly bored as he went through his carefully rehearsed spiel, but it was obvious that he really meant what he was saying. He'd merely said it too often.

Pointing at the virgin forest below, he said, 'This area is pretty much the same as it was in the days when the Indians roamed around in it. We like to think that's because of the work the National Park System's done.'

One of his passengers, the one with the bright pink shirt and the blue bow tie, asked, 'They're always trying to allocate more money for you characters. What do you really do to earn it? Stand around and watch the trees grow?'

Don fought down a tinge of anger. He was used to such carping, especially from locally oriented congressmen who begrudged every national dollar spent that did not result in additional industry and employment in their home district.

'We've had a camper explosion in the past few years,' Don said calmly. 'And that's good, because we want city people, or even rural people from other parts of the country, to see the good side of our forests. But they've got to be controlled.'

'You mean exploited, don't you?' asked Pink-Shirt.

His companion made a gesture of displeasure. He was a younger man, his face heavily sunburned. He had obviously been somewhere closer to the equator recently.

'Hold it down, Sam,' he said. 'No call to take off on this feller. He's only doing his job.' He leaned over and peered down into the green ceiling of the forest. 'How many folks charge in here every year, anyway?'

'It keeps going up,' Don said. 'Last season, we hit almost half a million. About the same this year, but because of the warm weather, we're getting a lot of post-season visitors. I'd guess we might see six hundred thousand.'

'At a couple of bucks apiece gate fee, and those rip-off prices for food at the lodge, you do pretty good,' grumbled Pink-Shirt.

'I'm paid by the Park Service,' said Don. 'If you want to take a look at my check after they get through with the deductions, you'll understand why there aren't many married rangers.'

Pink-Shirt made a low chuckling noise. 'Why bother?' he said. 'When you've got local talent like that little babe I saw this morning.'

'Sam,' warned his companion.

Don Stober said, keeping his voice under control, 'There are quite a few female rangers now. Something to do with equal rights.'

'Yeah, man,' said Pink-Shirt.

His companion hurried to ask, 'Is it getting out of hand? By making the wilderness so available, are we going to end up wiping it out?'

Gratefully, Don answered, 'That's what worries us. The parks belong to all the people. But when all the people try to use them—and mostly at the same time, those three months in the summer when the kids are out of school—it just won't work. They have a devastating effect on the habitat. We spend most of our time protecting the water, the fish, the wildlife, against the hundreds of thousands of people who turn up—most of them not knowing the first thing about getting along in the woods.'

'So set up a quota,' said Pink-Shirt. 'We're already spending too much money on this nonsense.'

'I think nonsense is the wrong word,' said the younger man. 'I just got back from the Caribbean. There's a blight destroying the palm trees there. The beaches look like the day after the invasion of Iwo Jima. Nothing but bare trunks sticking up into the sky. It could have been avoided. But nobody would spend the first dime.'

Don said, 'And who would enforce the quota? How can you tell a citizen—and taxpayer—that there's part of his country he isn't allowed to visit because he didn't make a reservation two years ago?'

Pink-Shirt stared down into the green canopy and said, 'Hold it!'

'Mister,' said Don Stober, 'You can't *hold* a chopper. Why?'

'I don't know,' said the older man. 'Forget it. I thought I saw something.'

'What?' Don asked.

'I'm not sure. It looked like some kind of big animal.'

'That's the idea of these parks,' said the younger congressman. He rubbed some sunburned skin off his nose. 'To give the animals some place to live.'

Up at the stream, June Hamilton heard the screams. At first, she thought that Maggie was putting her on, teasing her with a phony rape scene.

But that didn't last long. The intensity of the cries was too fearful, too raspingly agonizing.

Still, June hesitated. She felt the cold fingers of fear within her own vitals.

Then she abandoned caution and ran down the hill toward the camp site.

The first thing she saw was the violent movement as Maggie's body hurtled past her and crashed against a tree. The sound was sickening. Blood and air exploded from what had been, minutes before, a human being.

'Jesus!' shrieked the red-haired girl.

She felt something warm hitting her face. She reached up and when her fingers came down into view, they were laced with thick blood.

Her chest hurt. She had stopped breathing. Her fear was so great that she felt its leaden weight dragging her down into the soft forest floor.

Then the spell was broken.

She came face to face with the beast.

He had followed Maggie's body across the clearing, and as he reached for it, his giant head rose, and his eyes met those of the girl.

His nose lifted, and sniffed.

The blood scent came from this one.

He pushed Maggie's remains aside and started toward June.

She screamed, and ran.

The natural terrain and existing settlements had resulted in an unplanned gerrymandering of the park when its limits had been set up. On the map, the park appeared to be one giant square of bright green. But in reality, its boundaries were dictated by the rivers and streams, by the obstinate settlers who wouldn't sell their hundred and sixty acres to the Department of Interior, by access roads and the recommendations of wild game management experts.

So there were pockets which extended into the sides of the imaginary rectangle. And in one of these pockets, just a few hundred yards from the park itself, yet on private property, was the Wildhorse Mountain Lodge. The name of the lodge was in error, because Wildhorse Mountain was actually two slopes away. But where the lodge sat, the actual name was Squat Head Ridge, named after an Indian who had been killed there by one of the pony soldiers back during the Civil War Period, and who would want to spend thirty dollars a night to sleep in the Squat Head Inn?

Other than the name change, the builders of the lodge had done a good and honest job. Its facade was of split logs, erected more than half a century ago, and they had weathered well. This was hardly a town—it was more of an outpost—but the visitor who did not want to totally abandon civilization could find almost anything he needed in the way of creature comforts. There was a small market that carried most human needs from toothpaste to Pepto Bismol. Cans of spray deodorant lined its shelves, so that odor-conscious campers could help destroy the ozone layer. Instead of soap, high phosphate detergents were on sale to help choke the streams. Like most stores in the world, the Wildhorse Mountain market was a victim of mass merchandising.

Naturally, no such oasis would be complete without a bar, and the Inn had its own, a rustic, rough-hewn room complete with a life-sized painting of a semi-nude western lady of leisure. On the juke box, in addition to Tex Ritter, were such classics as 'El Paso' by Marty Robbins.

Although it was still early in the afternoon, the bar was

half-filled. Most of its inhabitants would never get any closer to the wilderness than the painting of Miss Sarah Keesler of Dutch Springs, Nevada. How the painting had found its way up this mountain was anybody's guess.

The bar, and indeed, the whole Inn, had a friendly kind of run-down quality that people liked. Nothing was actually dirty, or broken, but nothing was new and shiny either. This extended even to the appearance of the proprietor, Walter Corwin, a big man in his early sixties. Corwin, in this post-season period, had let most of his staff go—and was learning, as he did every post-season, that he wasn't really very good at dropping a tablecloth onto the table and having it float down neatly with all four corners squared. He tended to spill drinks while attempting to serve them, and his heavy hand was sure death to a plate of cheese. But his happy manner overcame the worst of his accidents, and people laughed along with him, rather than at him.

Allison Corwin, Walter's daughter, moved around the bar cleaning up after the lunch crowd. The smile she wore was warm, not the professional smirk of the harried waitress whose job she was filling. It would have been hard to guess her age. No one would have put her farther along than mid-twenties. Her actual years were more than that, but she still had the sexy and aggressive posture of youth. Just now, she was harried and hassled. At the season's end, Walter Corwin didn't like to invest in more glassware, and the highball glasses were down to the last case, thanks to a temperamental bartender who liked to throw them into the fireplace. She filled a tray and hurried behind the bar, began feeding the glasses into the automatic washer with its whirling brush and hot soapy water.

Walter Corwin looked around and frowned.

'You're washing glasses again? What did I tell you about that? Don't you ever listen to me?'

'All the time,' said Allison Corwin. 'Number one, you told me to always respect my father and mother. Which I did and do. And number two, you told me never to waste my precious mind, and the great thing about physical work is that you have lots of time to think. Number three, you—'

He interrupted. 'Enough! One of these days you'll stop wising off and listen.'

'I'm listening,' she protested. 'I'm listening!'

He looked around the bar. Nobody was close enough to overhear. 'Baby,' he said, 'I didn't know we'd get this busy, or I'd of kept Susy on. I can handle it. You came all this way to take pictures of people in the woods and up in the high country. So far, all you've gotten is dishpan hands. Why don't you unpack those expensive cameras and get to work before everybody heads back to the city?'

Washing another glass, Allison said, 'You're right, Pa. Absolutely right.'

'You're on your way to making it,' said her father. 'You got great reviews last time. What's the deadline for your new book?'

'Yesterday,' she said calmly.

He snatched up three of the glasses and began rinsing them. 'And you're up to your elbows in soap suds instead of—'

'Pa,' she said, 'don't start riding me too. My editor does enough of that. I only have a third of the book to go. I need maybe another thirty or forty good shots and I'm home free. I'm hoping snow will fall. I don't have enough snow stuff.'

'Publishers don't wait,' Walter Corwin warned. 'They're like sausage makers. They have to keep shoving that stuff out into the stores. They'll just move on without you.'

'I don't think so,' she said, aware that Kelly Gordon had just come in. He had taken off his peaked ranger hat, and carried it in his left hand.

Corwin did not see the ranger. He raised his voice. 'I run this place fine on my own, Allie. I don't need your help.'

She tried to signal him that they were being overheard, but he didn't notice. She said, 'You're under-staffed. You let your help go too soon this time.'

'Maybe so,' he said. 'But the glasses can wait. Your work can't.'

Kelly Gordon stepped up to the bar and said, 'Oh, Allison's an expert on letting work wait.'

She whirled on him, wordlessly. Allison Corwin had always been her own woman. She was used to fighting her own battles. But she had come to expect support and approval from Kelly. Now he seemed to be withdrawing it.

He looked directly at her and said, 'Maybe you ought to change your book's topic. Do one on how to avoid responsibility.'

'You—' she began. Then she remembered, and her face lost its angry tenseness. 'Oh, hell,' she muttered. 'I was supposed to meet you. Kelly, I'm sorry. I just got busy and—'

He put on the Charlton Heston face. Here, in the dim bar, it worked a little better. He teased, 'Listen, if dishes and dirty glasses are what you're into, don't let me stand in the way.'

Allison clinked one glass against the metal splashboard, nearly breaking it. She let it slip back into the water.

Tightly, she said, 'I've already got one father. I don't need two.'

'Well, do you need a ride up into the park?'

She hesitated.

Her father said, 'Get out of here, before you break all the profits. Go take some pictures.'

She dried her hands. 'All right. But don't complain to me when you run out of glasses right in the middle of the Happy Hour.'

'If I do, I'll use paper cups,' he said. 'You do your work, let me do mine.'

'All right,' she repeated. She wiped her hands again on a bar rag. She looked at Kelly. 'Let's split this scene while the sun is still working for me.'

'You need these,' said her father, holding out her gadget bag, bulging with cameras, lenses and film.

She took the bag and, impulsively, hugged him and kissed his weathered cheek.

Walter Corwin smiled at the couple. He liked Kelly

Gordon. And it was his private opinion that his daughter had been single long enough, professional photographer or not.

He waved at them as they left.

'Adios,' he called.

Kelly waved back. 'Adios, Walter.'

Kelly Gordon had taken the jeep Tom Cooper hadn't needed that morning. It was parked in the big lot outside the Wildhorse Mountain Lodge.

As they walked toward it, Allison Corwin said, 'It was sweet of you to drive down to get me. I'm sorry I forgot. I got busy and—'

'Bull,' said Kelly. 'This isn't the first time you've stood me up. I agreed to take you up to camp on company time, and now I've wasted the trip twice over. Did it ever occur to you that I might have been needed up there? Unlikely, but I just *might* have been.'

She put her arm around his waist as they walked and said, 'No excuse, sir. Guilty as charged.'

Kelly laughed. But he added, 'You know what's wrong with you? After your mother died, your father spoiled you rotten. And now you expect the same treatment from everybody else in the world.'

She stopped and his motion took him half a step past her. Her face wasn't angry, but her voice carried none of the teasing quality it had just shown.

'How long have you known me?' she asked.

'A few weeks,' he said, puzzled.

'That's not very long,' she said. 'Why don't you reserve judgment? Spoiled is a heavy word. It's a word I don't believe should be applied to me. First of all, I don't think I'm spoiled. I think I'm needed. My father has taken on a little more than he can handle at his age. I've been trying to help. In return, he indulges me and I enjoy it. But I don't demand it, and I don't believe it's automatically due me. Hell's bells, Kelly, haven't you ever been torn between two things? With me it's between my father's problems and my career. The career's still forming, but his problems are here right now. Which way do I go?'

Kelly said, 'I think Walter can handle his end of the deal. It's your end you should be worrying about. Or maybe it's easier this way? If you don't really try, you can't be blamed for failing.'

She tightened her lips. An angry retort came to them, but she choked down the words.

'I don't know,' she said. 'Look, give me some rope. I'll get it all together. I always do. Somehow.'

He shrugged, and got behind the jeep's steering wheel. She climbed in beside him.

As he ground the starter, she went on, 'Besides, I haven't really been leveling with Pa. He's got this thing about having a genuine book author in the family. Well, I got lucky with one book but all I've got going now is a feature story for that credit card magazine. Six hundred bucks and expenses.'

'Then you're wasting your time,' he said, as he drove out of the lot.

'Maybe. But I keep hoping I'll luck into a subject where I can really explore the graphics. The poets call it "finding your voice." That's what I need. A subject that will make me use everything I've got.'

Dryly, Kelly said, 'Good luck. But let me give you one word of advice from a non-professional.'

She softened, touched his arm.

'Give.'

'Cameras laying in the gadget bag don't take any pictures, good or bad.'

'You're right,' she said. Then, 'Forgiven?'

He said, 'Sure.' And added, 'But you were counting on that anyway, weren't you?'

Chastened, she said, 'Yes, I guess I was.'

'You're too late with too little,' said Kelly, piloting the jeep up the steep slope toward the ranger station.

'Pictures are my business,' said Allison Corwin, threading a 135mm telephoto lens into her Pentax. 'Driving is yours.

And if you don't watch yourself, you're going to drop us down into that gorge.'

'Like you said,' Kelly replied, 'driving's my business. And I've never skidded down into this gorge yet.'

Lifting the camera and peering through its viewfinder, Allison said, 'There's always a first time.'

June Hamilton did not know how long she had been running. Her headlong flight had turned into a series of stumbling lunges, and twice she fell and rolled down the steep slope until the unyielding bark of a tree stopped her with a thump.

The second time, she sat there for a moment, gasping. A sharp pain stabbed through her side.

Her eyes searched the forest, back the way she'd come.

Nothing. Not a bird, not a rabbit.

And not the beast.

'God,' she whispered. 'Oh, God. Please.'

She staggered to her feet and began to run again.

'You're going to break your neck,' Kelly Gordon yelled.

Allison Corwin squinted down at him through her Pentax.

'Smile,' she said. 'If you know how.'

'How much film do you burn up, anyway? I've counted six rolls already.'

'Seven.'

'Don't you ever stop shooting the same thing over and over?'

'Most of what I get can't be used. Wrong angle . . . wrong light. Wrong composition.'

Kelly touched his jaw. 'Wrong faces?'

She laughed. 'No. The faces are never wrong. That's what makes it good eventually.'

She scrambled down the eighteen-foot ladder.

'I thought you wanted to get some animal shots,' Kelly said. 'I'm supposed to be working.'

'You *are* working,' she said. 'Just go about what you normally do. Forget I'm here.'

He leaned over the saddle cinch he was repairing. 'I still think you picked the wrong face,' he said.

She moved in close and clicked off two more frames. 'Every face is a story, baby.'

'Baby?' he said. 'Have you been watching old Lauren Bacall movies again?'

'Hold still.'

'What kind of story do you think you get from my face?'

She lowered the camera. Her eyes met his.

'You're a dissembler.'

'Yeah,' he said. 'That's what I'm doing now to this saddle cinch. Dissembling it.'

'Oh, pooh! Stop kicking cow flop. And you'd better stop hiding everything behind that very tight jaw. One day it's going to break into a thousand pieces.'

He smiled.

'See?' she said. 'It's starting to crack already!'

June stumbled into the little clearing, crying with fear and exhaustion.

The old cabin had once been a line shack, for the riders who patrolled these forests when they were private property more than fifty years ago. It was faded dull gray by the wind and snow, and looked as if the next strong wind would knock it down. But to the terrified girl, it was like a welcoming fortress.

The door was jammed shut by the rusted hinges. She fought with the leather strap that served as a doorpull, broke it, almost wept with frustration, then managed to pry the door open far enough to get both hands on its edge. She put one foot against the wall and pulled with all her strength, and the rusty hinges wailed as they gave way.

She plunged into the gloomy interior and pulled the door shut behind her.

Sinking down in a corner, she began to choke, as she tried to calm her breathing.

Only now did she notice that her hands and arms were bleeding from the many scratches the sharp pine needles had scourged her flesh with as she plunged through the forest.

She hugged her knees close to her body and wept without sound.

It hadn't happened. It was only a wild freak-out, like she'd had the one time she had tried dropping acid. In a moment she would wake up and find herself safe in bed back in the rambling Lancaster Avenue house, the smell of coffee and frying eggs rich in the air.

But, as the chill air dried her sweat, and she began to shiver, she realized that this was reality; that Maggie lay dead up the mountain. Her weeping ceased. She had to think.

She was safe here. But night was coming on. She had to get down to the ranger station, down to other living human beings.

In a minute. Let me count to a hundred, and then I'll start down.

She had reached twenty-nine in her mumbled litany of numbers when the wall behind her gave a rippling motion and crashed inward, scattering broken boards across the single room of the cabin.

June started to scream, but the air was caught in her lungs and wouldn't come out. Her mind refused to believe this second assault. It spun away from her, retreating into fantasy.

Slowly, she stood and began to walk toward the closed door. Her voice came from a great distance. 'I'm going home,' she said. 'It's time I went home.'

She, mercifully, did not feel the giant claws as they ripped a huge chunk of flesh from her back. The impact staggered her, but the essence of spirit, of intelligence, that was really June Hamilton had escaped back to a warm bedroom where the aroma of coffee called her downstairs to breakfast.

When the second, destroying blow came, she was still walking slowly toward that remembered morning long ago.

Tom Cooper frowned at the low angle of the sun and

walked over to where Allison and Kelly were working.

'Kelly?'

'Yeah?'

'I think I'd better take the jeep up to R-Four.'

'That's horse country.'

'No time. I know a way to get up. I've got a couple of missing campers. Two girls. I saw them around noon and they said they'd be down before dusk.'

Kelly squinted at the golden sun, balanced like a ripe orange on top of the spruces. Allison caught the moment with a click of her shutter.

'They'll never make it now,' Kelly said. 'The sun's already sitting on the hilltops.'

'They're nice kids,' said Tom. 'Maybe they took a wrong turn and ended up over in Beaver Valley. It'd be a shame if they had to set up a dry camp.'

Kelly looked at his watch.

'We've got about half an hour. Okay, the jeep it is. And if you tear up the transmission, it comes out of your check.'

'Can I come?' asked Allison, reloading her camera. 'It sounds like fun.'

'Sure,' said Kelly, starting for the jeep. 'It'll be nice to see you taking pictures of somebody else for a change.'

The beast climbed the mountain slowly. The ache of hunger had abated.

Perhaps this side of the divide was a good place after all. Although the beast did not think in logical symbols, he had become aware that there was a new kind of food to be found here, food that was easy to acquire.

Even the pain from the shattered tooth had receded. He would find a place to sleep, and in the morning he would begin marking his territorial limits.

But now, back at the place where he had found the first food, there was something he must do.

'Let's hit Beaver Valley first,' said Kelly, at the wheel of the jeep, laboring up the trail which was little more than two ruts in the rock-littered slope. 'If they went down that way, chances are they holed up in that old line shack.'

'The light's going,' Allison complained. 'I'm going to have to switch to black and white.'

Kelly grinned. 'That must take all the joy out of it.'

'We'll see,' she said. 'Some people think black and white is the real test of a photographer.'

Tom Cooper pointed to a slashed blaze on a small birch tree. 'In that way,' he said. 'It's a short cut.'

'Oh?' said Kelly. 'Who's been blazing our timber?'

'Search me,' Tom said innocently. 'All I know is that's the shortest way to the line shack.'

'You'd be the one to know,' Kelly said. But he made the turn.

The road ended just below the weather-beaten shack. As they pulled up, Allison took several quick shots of it, silhouetted against the cloud-speckled sky.

'That shack's kept many a camper dry,' Kelly said.

Peering at it through her telephoto lens, Allison said, 'Well it looks like it could use a little help. What happened? Did somebody drive a bulldozer through it?'

Kelly parked the jeep and started up toward the cabin. Tom and Allison followed. Allison kept clicking away.

Kelly said, 'You're right. A whole wall's been knocked in. Tom, what the hell's been going on up here?'

'I came by last week,' Tom said. 'It was all right then.'

Kelly didn't wait for the others to catch up. He pulled open the door and went inside.

The darkness within made him stop for a second, until his eyes could begin to adjust. He looked right out the ruined wall into the forest, where the gloom of twilight was turning the hillside into a dank cavern.

The floor creaked under his feet, and the cabin trembled as he moved toward the shattered boards.

Something fell from the rafters. It draped over his shoulder and then slipped off. As it did, a mutilated hand scraped his cheek, covering his face with fresh blood.

Kelly leaped back. He did not exactly scream, but the

cry he gave was filled with rage and disgust.

He backed away from the thing on the floor, out the open door, and almost fell off the porch. Tom grabbed him.

Allison *did* scream. 'You're hurt!'

Kelly rubbed a gob of blood off his face. 'No,' he choked. 'Not me. Tom, get on the horn. We need some rangers up here right now. With flashlights and guns.'

Tom stared at him. 'Guns?'

'You heard me. Move!'

High up near the timber line, in a sheltered cave, the beast slept.

CHAPTER FOUR

Three husky rangers had hauled a small Honda gasoline-powered generator up the hill, and when it sputtered into action, bright lights glared across the R-Four campsite.

All of the rangers except Kelly were armed. Some had hand guns, but most carried heavy hunting rifles.

Into a walkie-talkie, Kelly said, 'How about it, Tom? Do you read me?'

'Roger,' came Tom Cooper's response.

'How far down are you?'

'We've worked our way up maybe a quarter of a mile from the cabin.'

'What do you see?'

'Not much. The girl's tracks; she came down the mountain like a bat out of hell. But nothing else.'

'No bear tracks?'

'Bear? Hell, I thought we were looking for puma or—'

'Negative,' said Kelly. 'Keep a sharp eye, Tom. I'm afraid we've got ourselves a rogue bear.'

'Ten-four,' said Tom. 'I'm clear.'

Kelly switched off the radio and looked around. The camp ground, illuminated by the harsh spotlights, had an unreal look to it. The lights did not penetrate into the trees, so the white birch trunks kicked back an effect of vertical bars, while the green spruces vanished into the darkness.

The blood, splashed over the tent and all the camping gear, was dark and seemed to be everywhere.

Allison moved quietly in the flood-lighted area, snapping pictures. Several of the rangers spoke to her, but she was so intent on her work that she made no response.

Something made a noise in the darkness, and a ranger threw his rifle up to his shoulder. Kelly almost leaped across the distance between them and knocked the muzzle down.

'Hold it!' he yelled. 'Make sure you know what you're shooting at.'

A ranger came out of the woods, sweating with the effort of his climb.

The first ranger lowered his rifle. 'Jesus!' he whispered. 'Thanks, Kelly.'

'Let's not get trigger-happy,' said Kelly. 'How about it, Larry. Did you see anything?'

'Exactly one hoot-owl,' said the sweat-stained ranger. 'Scared the crap out of me.'

'No tracks?'

'Just the girl's.'

'How far back are Tom and the others?'

'Five, ten minutes. They're spreading out. But it's darker than a witch's well in there, Kell. We might do better in the morning.'

'There were two girls,' Kelly said. 'We know where one is. The other might be out there hurt.'

'The way this place is ripped up?' said the ranger with the rifle. 'Kelly, there's more blood right here than I thought any one person could hold.'

'We keep searching,' Kelly said grimly. 'Fan out north of here. Maybe he went back up in the high country.'

'Are you sure there were two girls?' asked the ranger who had just come up the mountain.

'Tom talked to them this noon. There were two.'

'Maybe she got away?'

Kelly would have liked to believe that. But the evidence in the camp was too heavily weighted against it. 'No,' he said. 'But maybe when we find her, we'll find that rogue bear.'

'Then what?'

Kelly squeezed his eyes shut for a second. He did not want to say them, but the words had to come out.

'Shoot his goddamned head off.'

Half an hour later, Tom Cooper came out of the darkened forest. Kelly saw him first.

'Well?' he demanded.

'Nothing,' Tom said. 'Parker and Lane are right behind me, but they didn't find anything either.'

'Take a breather,' Kelly said. 'Then get your asses back in the woods. Nobody sleeps tonight until we get that bastard.'

Tom was surprised by the anger in Kelly's voice. Until now, there had been no ranger more devoted to the protection of the wild animals in the park.

'A bear's only a bear,' Tom said. 'He didn't know what he was doing.'

'That's no excuse,' Kelly grated. 'We're in trouble, Tom. There's a killer out there.'

'Are you sure it's a bear?'

'What else?'

'Mountain lion, puma, one of the big cats.'

'What cat could have knocked down that line shack wall?' Kelly shook his head. 'No, it's bear, and if we've been lazy in our garbage areas, Washington's going to fry our tails.'

'We haven't lured bear down with garbage since I've been here,' Tom said. 'And we police the visitors as best we can. But you can't stop them from feeding the bears. They think it's cute.'

'The newspapers aren't going to think it's cute, our letting two girls be killed and eaten by one of our bears.'

'Eaten?' said Tom, going pale. 'I didn't—'

'No,' said Kelly. 'You didn't see. And be glad you didn't. That poor thing back there in the cabin. . . . Tom, he scalped her. He ate every goddamned hair off her head.'

'My God,' Tom whispered, sickened.

Kelly heard the click of a camera's shutter, and realized that Allison was still taking photographs of them.

'I'm going to take her down the hill,' he said. 'This is no place for a woman. I'll get some chow and bring it up. You take over here, keep them circling in the forest. Two men together, armed. Be careful where you shoot, but if you come on that bear, blow him away.'

'Okay,' Tom said. In his mind, the image of the two

attractive girls he'd seen just hours before was being wiped away by a vision of a hairless, horrible thing chewed by fangs and torn by claws.

Allison had mounted one of her cameras on a small tripod, and was busy taking color time exposures of the camp site. She knew the moving men would emerge as streaking blurs on the finished transparency, but that was the effect she wanted, as she set the shutter to two seconds.

Kelly said, 'Come on, Allie. Get your gear together, and let's go. I'll take you down to the lodge.'

She yelped, 'You'll what? Kelly, don't you realize what we've got here? I've found a subject for my book.'

'It's going to be a long night,' he said.

'I don't mind. Come on, move. You're blocking my shot.'

'Okay,' he said. 'But stay out of our way too. There may be some real shooting.'

He went over to another ranger, instructed him to go down to the station for coffee and sandwiches, and began to supervise the gruesome task of gathering together the blood-covered back-packs and torn clothing that had belonged to the two girls.

Allison, who had been using a boulder as a seat, decided to move further away from the flood-lit area. She lifted the camera and moved around the big rock, into its shadow.

Her foot sank into suddenly porous ground. She drew back at first, surprised by the unexpected give to the earth.

But she had trouble pulling her foot out. Something warm and sucking seemed to surround her ankle.

At that moment, a ranger plugged in another bank of floodlights, and sudden brilliance illuminated what had formerly been in shadow.

Allison managed to move her foot. And as it came out of the surrounding earth, it brought with it bits of torn flesh and blood.

She screamed and threw herself over the boulder, knocking her camera to the hard rock and smashing its three-hundred-dollar 200 mm. lens.

Doctor Samuel Hallit was in charge of the High City clinic, which doubled as emergency ward and coroner's office. He had lived here for almost thirty years, and had taken on certain aspects of the hard, craggy mountains which surrounded the town. He was a small man, a bachelor who had never been tempted, a compulsive worker whose attention to minor detail was legendary. He was also one of the best doctors in the state.

His face was weathered by lines that resembled the crevices in the glaciers that crawled down from the big mountain. His hair and moustache were as white as the ice that hung from the rock outcroppings. And, from so small a man, his voice came like the howl of the January wind.

The bodies of both girls were on examination tables, draped with coverings. But blood clotted through the cloth.

Dr. Hallit finished washing his hands.

'Bear?' Kelly persisted. He had asked the question four times, and four times during the examination, Hallit had brushed it aside.

'I had to be sure,' said the doctor. 'Yes, bear. And a big one. I've never seen such damage.'

'How big?'

'Big as a grizzly, at least. Kelly, you don't have any grizzlies in the park, do you?'

'No.'

'Well, one of your blacks must have gone crazy. Or maybe it was a sow, with cubs, and these girls got too close. Might even have tried to take the cub home.'

'Cubs would have left sign,' Kelly said. 'We didn't find a trace. In fact, we didn't even find any bear sign.'

'Bad mannered sort,' said Hallit. 'Ate and ran.'

Kelly didn't appreciate the joke. Death was a closer companion, apparently, to Dr. Hallit than to the ranger.

He said, 'We hauled ever goddamned bear in the park up to the high country this spring. Why would one come down now?'

'To find food,' said the doctor.

'There's plenty of food up there. The streams are brimming with fish.'

'Maybe this one got tired of fish.'

'Doc, I'm in no mood for sick jokes.'

'This isn't a joke, Kelly. Your bear was hungry enough to kill those two girls and eat them. You saw what was left.'

'Yeah,' Kelly said. 'But bears don't eat people.'

'This one did,' said Hallit.

Kelly shook his head. 'It's a mess. Listen, do me a favor. Put this all down in your report? We're going to have ourselves one hell of a public relations problem.'

Hallit nodded. 'And your first one is going to be assigning some poor bastard to call the victims' families.'

Kelly looked at the floor. He said, 'I couldn't stick anyone with that one. I guess I'm the poor bastard you mentioned.'

Hallit sighed. 'It's a crummy world sometimes.' He slid open a desk drawer and took out a flat bottle. 'Here. I keep this for those occasions when the world is too much with me.'

Kelly took a welcome swig, and choked.

As he handed back the bottle, the door opened, and a well-dressed man in his late forties hurried in. He was slim, with a pale face that saw no more of the sun than could hit him as he hurried from his office to his automobile.

He sniffed the aroma of the good brandy.

'Drinking, Kelly? On duty?'

'Mr. Kittredge,' Kelly said patiently, 'It's nearly midnight. I went off duty at five. I'm working on my own time right now.'

'Oh, all right,' said the park supervisor. While Kelly Gordon had effective control of the day-to-day operation of the park, Avery Kittredge had the title on his door. He was anything but popular with the field rangers; the previous director had spent more time on horseback and climbing ridges than he did indoors. But that wasn't Kittredge's style. He was handier with a memo than a mule prod. 'Why wasn't I notified of this appalling accident?'

Kelly said, 'We called your home and left a message. You weren't at either of your clubs.'

'I had a speaking engagement,' Kittredge said harshly.

'Well, you're here,' Kelly said. 'Obviously, one way or the other, you got the word.'

'Yes,' Kittredge said angrily. 'I got it on the radio, head-lined in the news. Why wasn't the report held back until I approved it?'

'Because,' Kelly replied loudly, 'We don't want any climbers heading up into the high country until we get the situation under control.'

The doctor cleared his throat, looked at his watch. 'If you gentlemen will excuse me? I have quite a lot of work ahead.'

He nodded toward the two examination tables.

For the first time, Kittredge saw the bloodied clothes covering the terribly still bundles of deformed flesh. His face whitened.

'Thanks, Doc,' Kelly said. 'We were just leaving, weren't we, *Mr.* Kittredge?'

Kittredge made a choking sound and almost ran from the room.

'Don't push it, son,' warned the doctor.

'I'll try,' said the ranger. He went out into the night, and found the supervisor leaning against the porch, making gagging sounds.

Kelly turned away. It wasn't fair to watch any man at such a moment.

But Kittredge sensed his presence and whirled.

'Hold it, Kelly!' He managed to regain his composure. 'Let's have it. What the hell happened up there?'

Kelly tried to keep it loose. 'We're still searching. But it looks like one of our bears got lonesome up in the high country, and came down looking for some real action.'

Kittredge snapped, 'I suppose you think that's funny.'

'No, I don't. But what the hell good does it do to stand around crying?'

'Well?' demanded the supervisor. 'What are you doing about it?'

'I've got men up in the field tracking him down, and we've put R-Three and R-Four off limits to campers. I think he's in one of those areas, and with luck we can contain him there.'

'I want hourly reports,' said Kittredge.

Kelly scowled. 'Really? Do you want us calling you every hour on the hour all night?'

Kittredge realized the insanity of his request. 'Well ... no. But keep me informed all the way.'

Kelly crawled into the Toyota. The jeep was still up on the mountain. Kittredge had followed him over. 'And keep this in mind, Kelly. After this is over, I want an investigation.'

'Investigation? What kind of investigation?'

'We have a responsibility to the public.'

'And we carry it out. We've had a perfect safety record.'

'Until *tonight!* Don't snow me, Kelly. It's my head on the block. How could this happen? Those bear are supposed to be in the high country.'

'That's where we put them,' said the ranger. 'But remember, we don't have any fences up that way.'

'Granted,' said Kittredge. 'One of them may have come down. Or maybe you didn't do your job. Maybe you didn't move them all.'

Kelly said, 'We tagged every goddamned bear in the park. Ask Arthur Scott. He knows every bear in this forest by first name. There's no way we could have missed one.'

'Now, that's a good idea you just had,' Kittredge said. 'Get hold of Scott. Get him down here. I want to talk with him.'

Kelly turned the key and the Toyota's engine turned over.

Kittredge hardened his voice. 'Kelly, I hope you don't think I've been talking to myself.'

'No,' said Kelly Gordon. 'I read you loud and clear.'

He mashed down the gas pedal and left Avery Kittredge fuming in a cloud of smoke and scattered gravel.

CHAPTER FIVE

The beast, unaware that a massive search had been started to track him down and kill him, awoke in his shelter and gave a contented yawn. His belly was still full, and dimly he was aware that he had stumbled on a rich source of food that seemed inexhaustible. Until now, the two-legged ones had been only vague enemies, to be avoided and hidden from. But now that he had learned they were red meat, the beast had lost all fear of their strange scent and noisy ways.

He had never heard a gun fired, or seen an arrow launched. He had no way of knowing that these weak creatures had powerful ways to protect themselves.

So, as he rolled and scratched in the first gray light of dawn, his mind turned to the juicy, easy food he had discovered, and his crafty mind began to form a plan of action.

Don Stober whirled the helicopter through the still morning air. With him, as observer, Gail Nelson scanned the forest below with field glasses. She had insisted on taking her regular shift in the chopper patrol against Tom's wishes.

'Nothing,' she reported. 'Not a thing is moving.'

'It's early yet,' he said. 'Keep your eyes open.'

'I will,' said the young ranger. 'How awful for those poor girls.'

'They won't be the last,' Don said grimly. 'Not unless we luck into finding that bear.'

'How can you say that?' she said. 'It was just an accident.'

'He's tasted blood,' he told her. 'From now on, he'll be a killer. Until we kill him.'

He shoved the yoke to one side and the Hughes chopper banked violently and slipped around the edge of a steep cliff.

Although only two camping areas had been closed off, the word of the killings spread through other areas, and by mid-morning, a mass exodus from the woods had begun.

Back-packers streamed down from the low-slope areas they'd been exploring. In more congested areas, tents were struck—often by cutting the tie ropes rather than waste time in pulling up the stakes.

The rangers, most of whom had only managed to grab an hour or so of sleep, were anything but popular this morning. The general attitude seemed to be that they were somehow responsible for what had happened.

It would take days to restore the camp sites to their original condition.

But, somehow, that didn't seem very important just now.

To a ranger, the rifle is an enemy except for authorized practice and licensed hunting. To a man, they have come upon too many wounded and slaughtered animals abandoned by careless hunters, many taking game out of season, to appreciate the loudly declared right of every citizen to bear arms. Many citizens should not even be allowed to drive a car, let alone aim a high-powered weapon.

But the rangers on the sides of the mountain this morning all carried rifles, and chambered in them were soft-nosed, expanding 30.06 220-grain slugs, which hit with more than two tons impact and blew up inside the body of the target. Even this was considered lightweight ammunition when going up against an enraged bear.

Today, the rifle was a welcomed tool . . . an implement that might save a ranger's life before the day was over.

Not all campers had fled the park. Some welcomed the 'adventure.'

In one high country site, near the edge of R-Three, two young back-packers sat, sipping beer, and listening to a transistor radio.

The announcer said, 'Today there's news of another tragic accident—this one in the National Park. Most years, we hear of unnecessary deaths caused by careless campers. This year has been free of such mishaps. But now a double death has been caused up near the timber line by what appears to be a rogue bear. Two young women were slain by a beserk bruin, and the official opinion is that they may have appeared to threaten a bear cub and were killed by the angry mother. Search teams are on the move, and the hopes are they will either capture or kill the bear shortly. Private sources say the young women were so badly mutilated that the evidence points toward a dangerous animal—a killer bear, using all its cunning and wiles to destroy the enemy . . . man.'

Tom Cooper, riding Tex, paused near the edge of the clearing.

He addressed the two young men. 'Hey, guys. Didn't you get the word about evacuating this area?'

'We just got in,' said one camper. 'You mean about that bear?'

'Yeah. I know it's a hassle, but we've got to move everybody out of this area until we bring that rascal down. He's killed two girls already.'

'Hell,' said the other camper. 'Bears don't hurt you unless you mess with them. We hiked all the way up here and we just spent an hour pitching our tent.'

'Sorry,' said Tom. 'Areas one and two down the mountain are safe. Set your rig up there.'

'Sure they're safe,' said the first camper. 'They're filled with noisy brats and TV sets at full blast. What bear in his right mind would ever head that way? No thanks.'

'Well, mister,' Tom said, hardening his voice, 'You just don't have any choice.'

The camper finished his beer can, almost threw it into the woods, and saw Tom watching. Instead, he stowed it in a black plastic garbage bag.

'On your way down,' Tom added, 'Make a lot of noise. You don't want to surprise any bears. Give them plenty of warning you're coming, and they'll usually move away. They're very dangerous if you jump them.'

'Yeah, sure,' said the second camper. 'Okay, Harry, let's break camp.'

'Wait a minute,' said the other. He went over and stroked Tex's neck. To Tom, as if they were old friends, he said, 'Listen, pal, we planned on this trip for months. Why don't you just forget you found us here? We know our way around in the woods. We're not afraid of your bear.'

'Sorry,' said Tom. 'I can't do that.'

Henry took out a twenty-dollar bill and rolled it around his finger.

'Maybe this might help loosen up your memory?'

Tom stared at the camper for a long moment, his jaw tensing with anger. Then, without a word, he dismounted, walked over to the tent and pulled up one of the corner stakes by its rope. The tent collapsed like the skin of some giant green creature.

The two campers gaped at the ranger.

Tom remounted his horse. 'Mister,' he said softly, 'You just broke camp. And you've got exactly fifteen minutes to police up this area and get down the trail.'

He waited to see if there would be an argument. There wasn't any. Henry slipped the twenty-dollar bill into his pocket furtively and turned to his partner.

'Come on,' he said loudly. 'You heard the man. We don't have all day.'

Kelly Gordon's office at the ranger station was simple and almost militarily neat. The desk was old, of battered wood. The chairs were even older, and did not match each other. One file cabinet was taller than the other. The office looked exactly like what it was—a collection of furniture scavenged from various other offices.

The narrow screened windows fronted on a vista of trees and mountains that would have been breathtakingly beautiful if anyone in the office had ever bothered to look through them. But this was a place for business, not sightseeing, and right now, Kelly was all business.

Speaking into the telephone, he raised his voice. 'Okay, I read you. Mr. Scott is not in the office. That's no surprise. He's never in the office. He's always out in the woods wearing one of his cock-eyed costumes. But this is an emergency. Use your radio to connect me with him.'

He waited for an answer, and didn't like it when the voice of a young man said, 'I'm sorry, sir. I can't do that.'

Kelly said, 'What are you saying? That you can't connect me with Scott, or you *won't*?'

'Technically I could,' the voice replied. 'But Mr. Scott left strict instructions. He wasn't to be contacted unless it was a major emergency.'

'Sonny,' Kelly said grimly, and now his voice fought to hold down the anger that wanted to spew out. He lost the battle. 'You just listen to me. We brought in the bodies of two young girls who were eaten to the bone by one of our animals. So don't throw snow about "major emergencies". This qualifies as one, and if you don't get me Scott on that radiophone in the next minute, you're going to be standing in the unemployment line tomorrow morning.'

The voice hesitated. 'I didn't know. I'm sorry. I'll try to raise Mr. Scott. Hold the line.'

'That's better,' said Kelly. 'I'll be here.'

As he waited, the door to his office opened and Allison came in. He gave her a little wave.

Her return gesture was slow. 'Hi,' she said.

'Are you all right?' he asked.

'As right as I can be on a strict Valium diet.'

'You didn't eat?'

She sat on the corner of the desk. 'I don't think I'll eat for maybe another year. Or sleep. I kept coming awake with their faces staring at me—'

Her voice was on the verge of trembling. She brought it under control by finding something else to talk about. She pointed at the big map of the park on the wall. It had several red and blue-headed pins stuck in at different locations.

'What's with the pins in the map?'

Kelly said, 'The red pins show where we found the girls. The blue ones are places where I think our animal may have gone off to digest his meal.'

'Animal? Then you still aren't sure it was a bear?'

He said, 'Nearly sure. But there's still the faint possibility that—' He broke off the sentence, said into the phone: 'Yes?'

The other voice said, 'I'm ringing Mr. Scott now.'

To Allison, Kelly said, 'Sit down, this'll only take a minute.' Into the phone: 'I'm holding, son. Keep on ringing until he answers.'

The voice said, ruefully, 'Yes sir. But I hope you explain to him that you made me do it. Mr. Scott's not going to be very happy about this.'

'Don't worry,' Kelly promised. 'I'll get you off the hook.'

Few modern humans have ever seen a herd of big-horned elk close up with the naked eye. If the white-tailed deer is considered nervous and shy, the elk is a wild-eyed paranoid about his privacy. Where many of the park animals had become accustomed to humans, and even tolerated them, the elk left the paths of man strictly alone.

The small herd here in a high altitude clearing were miles from the nearest road, and not even a foot trail came anywhere close to this place. Still, the huge buck who led the herd kept his head turning, his wide nostrils sniffing the air for alien scent. The does and young calves grazed while he kept watch.

Once, his great head lifted and he stared, with his four-power binocular vision, at a shape that stood near the edge of the clearing, just within the forest. He sniffed, but the acrid scent of man did not seem present. For a moment he waited, alert to any movement that might be hostile.

But none came. Satisfied that the furred thing within the trees was not an enemy, he lowered his head again and grazed. But one eye was always turned toward the forest.

The bundle of furred hides stirred slightly. The movement did not go unnoticed by the elk, but it did not alarm him.

Within the hides, strapped around him like a giant deer pelt, a man smiled. His lips moved soundlessly. A lip-reader would have seen the word, 'Good' formed on them.

Then a harsh 'Beep' shattered the calmness of the quiet clearing. The elk herd reacted by freezing all motion. For a fraction of a moment, they became living brown statues, poised for flight, yet avoiding movement that might attract a preying eye.

The man inside the hides mumbled a curse and made a grab for the two-way radio in its holster strapped to his belt. He was too late. The harsh 'Beep!' came again.

This time, the elk herd was energized into frantic movement. The buck leaped first, covering more than twenty feet from a standing start. The rest of the herd followed him, and in seconds the clearing was empty and still.

Arthur Scott threw off his fur hides and yanked the offending radio from its holster. He whipped up the antenna, pressed the transmit button and shouted, 'What the hell is the matter with you, Barney? I gave you strict orders not to contact me. Do you know what you've—'

The young man's voice said, 'I'm sorry, but Kelly Gordon said it was an emergency. He insisted—'

'Oh?' snarled Scott. 'Kelly *insisted?* Well, put him on, I'll insist him!'

'I'm on,' said Kelly. 'Listen, Scotty, we've got ourselves a problem—'

'*You've* got a problem,' Scott yelled into the radio. 'Do you know what you just blew for me? A whole week's work!'

Kelly tried to cut in, but Scott kept shouting, 'I had me a family of elk. I've been on their trail all week, moving with them, damned near living with them. I've seen behavior that—'

'Damn it, will you shut up and listen?' Kelly finally managed to say. 'We've had a bear killing.'

'That's the end of my elk this season,' Scott went on. Then what Kelly had said sank in. 'We've had a *what?*'

'Two women were killed late yesterday. Up in R-Four. I think it was a bear. And that means it was probably one of *our* bears, Scotty.'

'Nonsense,' said Arthur Scott into the radio. 'None of our

bears would attack unless they were really provoked. Even then, they'd probably maul, rather than kill. Besides, our bears are all up in the high country.'

'Tell that to Kittredge,' Kelly said. 'He's holding you and me responsible. He as much as came out and said we faked the bear move, that we didn't really move them up there at all.'

'That man is an idiot,' Scott said calmly. 'He's more of a paranoid than my herd of elk.'

'Be that as it may,' Kelly said, 'We've got to come up with some action and some answers. So forget your elks and get your tail down here on the double.'

'Okay,' said Scott. 'End transmission.'

'Ending transmission,' said the young man's voice.

'You do that thing, sonny,' Kelly said. He hung up the phone.

Allison asked, 'Who's Scott?'

'A hot-shot naturalist who's been temporarily attached to the park. He's working on some kind of long-term study of the wildlife here. He's really good. He sprays himself down with some kind of gunk to kill the human odor, and wraps himself up in a bunch of deer hides. Next thing you know, he's right there in the middle of an elk herd, eating grass with them. As for bears, there's not one in the whole park Scotty doesn't know personally.'

Allison managed her first laugh since the events at the cabin the evening before. 'You're kidding.'

'Not a bit. If you're serious about going through with a photo book on this mess, you'd do worse than to follow Scotty around for a while. I've never met a man who knew more about animals, or could get along better with them.'

She studied him. Somehow his face today was different. Perhaps it was the double tragedy up the mountain; perhaps just a sleepless night. But he had lost much of the carefree quality of adventure that had first attracted her. She didn't know which Kelly she liked better; yesterday's or today's.

She said, 'You guys really love what you're doing up here, don't you? It's more than just a job.'

'It had better be,' he said. 'Nobody in his right mind would work for what they pay us.'

'Why do you?'

'Some of the younger guys like it because it's a good summer job, a way to be outdoors and get paid for it. A few of them are nature freaks, they think they're all that stands between what we've got here and total destruction of the environment.'

'Neither category fits you.'

He gave a short laugh. 'I guess I came up here to get back in touch with basic realities.'

'But you stay while the others go home after a summer or two.'

He shrugged. 'Let's say that the reality up here is habit-forming.'

'Sometimes people acquire one habit to break another one.'

He nodded. 'I'll buy that. After I got back from the war, I went off on a tangent for a while. Acquired the wrong values. The wrong people.'

'Oh? Was one of those acquisitions a wife?'

'Was she ever.' He went over to the steaming Silex. 'You want some coffee?'

'Thanks.'

He poured two cups and gave one to her. He stood, looking out the narrow window, sipping at it. 'I had a lot of habits that needed breaking. And coming up into these mountains was one way to do it.'

'What about her?'

'She's doing well, I hear. In fact, she was doing well when I met her. She's happy.'

'Is she beautiful?'

He nodded. 'And rich. One of the directions I went off base was in wanting money. She had it and was willing to share. That simple.'

Allison warmed her hands on the coffee cup. 'It's never that simple.'

'Let's say we were both mercenaries. Out for something

the other had. We devised little face-saving methods of avoiding that cut-and-dried a description. I was getting set up in the real estate business, and that takes time and money. I had the time, and she had the money.'

Allison looked away. 'I see.'

He put down his cup. 'Do you? I don't think it's something you can really understand until you've been through it yourself. Remember, we weren't two stockbrokers trading in futures. We thought we had a good thing going. But it turned sour, or maybe it always was, and it took me five years to find out. By then, I was making a good buck with my agency, and I guess it was the realization that I really didn't *need* her in the same way that triggered the decision that I didn't need her at all.'

'Very noble of you,' said Allison, stiffly. 'How about her? Did she need you?'

'She thought she did. That's more or less the same thing, isn't it?'

'But you left her anyway?'

'No. Give me some credit. I didn't leave. I simply behaved like a heel. I pretended I was having an affair.'

She raised an eyebrow. '*Pretended?*'

He made a rueful grin. 'That's all, baby. In fact, it's all I was capable of. Because those five years had done something to me that you read about in all those magazine articles about sex therapy. I was as impotent as the harem eunuch.'

She rolled her eyes in mock despair. 'Now he tells me!'

He chuckled. 'Oh, the problem's all gone. In fact, it went away just a week or so after she filed for divorce.'

'So the phony affair worked.'

'Not on you life. In fact, it turned her on. She started wearing her sheer nighties again and taking perfume showers.'

'And?'

'And nothing. So I sold out my holdings, donated the whole pile to charity, and enrolled in Ranger school. It was a master stroke. She was turned off instantly, and headed for Reno.'

Allison shook her head slowly. 'You lie in your teeth,' she said. 'Why?'

'Why do you think?'

She considered that for a moment. Then she stood and came closer to him.

'I think what you're trying to do is turn *me* off.'

He looked down at her. 'Why would I do that?'

'Because you're afraid. Because you were hurt, and you're afraid of being hurt again.'

'Nobody wants to get hurt.'

'No,' she said. She touched his face. 'You don't have to be afraid, Kelly. We come in all shapes, sizes and colors. Just because your first order from the catalog didn't fit isn't reason to give up. Try another page.'

'Maybe I will,' he said.

Their bodies were close together.

Later, he would not remember who reached out first. All he could recall was their pressing together in a greedy embrace, and the little nibbling kisses she gave him that gradually subsided into a warm, deep one that left him trembling as he pushed her away.

Hoarsely, he said, 'No hanky-pank in the office.'

She bit the skin on the back of his hand gently.

'Still afraid?' she asked.

'Ask me that tonight,' he said.

She bit a little harder. 'That's a date.'

CHAPTER SIX

The beast, well-fed and drowsy, was becoming uneasy.

There was a new rhythm to the movement in the forest. The hated smell of men and machines was stronger, and the beast's keen ears heard the rustle of activity along the many trails on this side of the mountain.

The cave seemed more like a trap now than a retreat, so the beast abandoned it.

Despite his great size, the beast could move through the trees like a whisper, leaving little or no trace of his passing. At intervals, he would stop and mark the trees with his tearing claws, reaching up as high as he could to make the bark-shredding sign that this was his territory. Vaguely, he realized that while others of his kind would observe such markings, the two-legged ones ignored them.

Suddenly, there was more than hunger within him. He had fed well, and did not have the urge to eat again.

But his own version of anger began to swell inside his chest. He began to form a vague emotion toward the two-legged ones that might be described as hatred.

As he moved, the beast tried to stay at the high elevations he preferred. But as he cut more and more trails that bore the spoor of men, he turned away from them, and this forced him downward, gradually, until he was in the thickest part of the forest.

There, he drank from a stream, and watched with amusement as three trout sped toward the safety of a submerged rock pile.

The beast had no more interest in fish.

The two rangers moved slowly up along the stream's edge. The sun reached here, and they were both sweating. Dark moisture stained the small of their backs.

The deep odor of balsam and blue spruce filled the air.

In the woods themselves, the humus which had fallen from the pines would be so thick it would be like wading in pillows to walk upon it. But along the edge of the rapidly cascading stream, the ground was relatively clear, except for the last growths of wild sarsaparilla and glacier lily. Inside the forest itself would be long strands of grizzly hair, a lichen that grows, parasitically, from the trees, like Spanish moss in the deep south, and springing overnight from the forest floor giant mushrooms would open their white umbrellas.

The mountainside was a feast of beauty, one that Gail Nelson never tired of enjoying.

But today's hike was not for pleasure. She, and the other ranger, Tom Cooper, each carried rifles. Gail's was a .308 caliber Winchester with the short barrel and a lever action. It was a good brush gun, thanks to the short length which was less likely to foul in undergrowth, and the heavy slug would clip through most branches without being turned aside. Tom had his old sporterized Springfield '03, with a four-power Redfield scope on it. It was more of a long-range weapon than Gail's, so between them, they were well armed.

They stopped on a point where gravel jutted out into the stream bed.

'Damn,' gasped the girl. 'You can never find a bear when you need one.'

'We're in Area Three,' Tom said, trying to keep his voice steady and failing. It had been a hard climb. 'I don't think he's come down this low.'

'We could be walking right past him,' Gail said. 'The woods are so thick he could be twenty yards away and we'd never see him.'

'I don't think so,' Tom disagreed. 'We'd see some sign, hear him—maybe even smell him. This time of year, they're pretty gamey.'

'Maybe,' she said. 'I'll give you this much, it's hard to believe he's down here, because my hot little feet have stepped on every square inch of this forest floor.'

'Tired?'

'Beat.'

He looked at his watch. 'Why don't you take a break? I want to check out Powder Ridge, but it doesn't need both of us.'

'It's a deal,' Gail said gratefully. 'Remind me to do you a favor some time.'

'How about tonight?' he suggested. 'We missed last night because of all the excitement.'

'Is that a proposition?' she asked.

'Do you want it to be?'

She gave a little chirp of laughter and said, 'You bet your sweet patootie.'

'I'll be back in fifteen, twenty minutes,' he said. He turned and hurried up the trail. Because he knew that if he didn't leave right now, Powder Ridge might never get checked out.

Gail leaned back against a rock and smiled.

Well, why not? It had been a long summer during which she had been a very good girl. Well, almost very good. There had been that young mountain climber from England. But on the job, she had been the model of proper behavior.

The season was over. It wouldn't hurt to loosen up a little.

Besides, with what had happened to those girls yesterday, you suddenly realize that nobody guaranteed you seventy years and smooth sailing all the way. It could come to a horrible, bloody end around the next corner. Have some fun while you can, Gail baby.

From her helicopter ride with Don Stober this morning, she remembered there was a waterfall just around the next curve of the stream. That might be pleasant, listening to it while she waited for Tom.

Slowly, she made her way up along the edge of the stream. The sun was warm and golden. It was good to be alive on a day like today.

The beast had never smelled perfume before. Those two he had taken yesterday had been in the woods for almost a week, and the strong soap they'd used for bathing left a fatty, animal-like odor on their bodies.

But this one exuded a scent of something like the glacier flowers he had nibbled in the spring and summer. The slight odor excited the beast, and he followed carefully, stalking without sound and without hurry.

The waterfall was bigger than it had seemed from the air. It cascaded down almost twenty feet, dancing and shimmering like a liquid curtain. The pool beneath was deep and crystal clear. In its depths, Gail could see one Dolly Varden trout that must have weighed almost twenty pounds. These 'bull trout,' as the old timers called them, made good eating and better sport in catching. It was too bad fishing wasn't allowed in the park. She would have liked to cast a lure down toward the bottom and watch the trout to see if it appealed to him.

She checked the safety on her rifle, and leaned it against a boulder. The waterfall, just feet away, whispered an invitation to her.

She resisted it. She would just slip off her boots and soak her feet for a moment.

The water was cold, but exhilarating. Funny. A cold shower was a turn-off, good only for waking up in the morning, or damping down too-horny boy friends who wanted everything, all at once and too fast.

But the thought of a cold shower under a mountain waterfall . . . that sent a little tingle up her back.

Of course, she couldn't. Tom would be coming back any moment.

She splashed her feet in the water, and the big trout gave her a cool look, speculating on whether or not those white things dangling into his pool might be good to eat.

They splashed again, and he moved closer. So close that his sleek side brushed against Gail's toes, and she gave a little shriek and leaped back.

Behind her, in the bushes, she heard a sound that was a mixture between a sigh and a low snort.

Tom! As in Peeping! He hadn't gone up to Powder Ridge after all.

She felt a warm glow spreading across her lower body.

Why not? It had been coming for a long time. What better place than here, in the beauty of this secret glade, with its dancing waterfall? It would be a far better memory than the sweaty sheets of a furtive motel.

She slipped out of her clothing quickly, making an obvious point of ignoring the bushes behind her. She was proud of her body. Once, a photographer who claimed he was from *Playboy* offered her two hundred dollars for a nude session. Being photographed that way gave her a tiny thrill of excitement, but it vanished when he put down his camera and grabbed for her with both hands. She had wrapped a robe around her, grabbed her clothing, and fled down the hall of the office building to a toilet where she'd changed, left the robe, and slipped out without her model's fee. A call to the magazine revealed the man was an imposter, an all-too-common happening, the nice lady on the magazine's staff sighed. By the time she'd decided to report the 'photographer' to the police, he had vanished from the 'studio' which turned out to be rented by the week to anyone with thirty dollars.

But she still liked to be looked at, and it pleased her to think of Tom watching her now. She hoped it would thrill him too. Maybe he would join her under the waterfall.

The sun caught the highlights in her tawny blonde hair, giving it a golden, almost honey-like color. She lowered her jeans without embarrassment; she was a natural blonde, all the way, and for some odd reason this was almost as exciting to those few men she had known as the fact of her nakedness.

She piled her clothing on the boulder, near the rifle. She could sense eyes upon her. She smiled, and stepped into the rushing water, feeling gingerly along the bottom to avoid the sharp rocks that waited there.

The cold water struck her shoulders and back with a chilling impact that made her cry out in delicious near-pain. She found, to her surprise, that there was a kind of cavern behind the cascading water, and she slipped back into it while she got her breath. The water, in front of her, made a shimmering wall, half transparent, half opaque.

Gail sensed movement, and her body tingled. Goose-bumps broke out, from a combination of the chill air and anticipation of what was to come.

A shadow moved to, then through, the dancing wall of water.

She gave a giggle and said, 'You sure got undressed quick.'

The big Dolly Varden trout swam in agitated circles. This pool, which was his home, had its rhythms and cycles, but all were known to the killer trout, who defended its waters against all other male Vardens. The sight or scent of blood was nothing new to the fish; many final battles had been fought in the pool, between fish or small mammals such as muskrat or water shrews.

But now the pool was being flooded with a torrent of crimson that clouded the water with its swirling tendrils. It flowed—almost cascaded—from the ledge where the waterfall beat against the surface of the stream, coming in gushing torrents until the Dolly Varden flicked his tail and sped downstream to a place where the water was still fresh and clear.

CHAPTER SEVEN

There are still many who believe that the insolent chariots sold by Detroit can go anywhere and surmount any terrain. This attitude may come from the first years of automobile driving, when cars were indeed able to take to the woods and follow deer paths. But those early Model A Fords, those Tin Lizzies, had high road clearance, and weighed only a quarter of present-day vehicles. Nor did they carry such rock-snagging undergear as mufflers, torsion-bar suspension or low-slung oil pans. One old-timer who passed on in 1924 had actually stipulated in his will that his Model A be buried with him because, in his own words, 'I ain't never got into a hole that she couldn't get me out of.'

While the main roads in the park were of decent asphalt construction, many of the dirt roads going up to the remote camp sites were more like dry creek beds, filled with ruts, rocks and exposed tree roots. A Model A might have sputtered its way up them with little difficulty, but even an off-road jeep had trouble here and there.

As for the visitors, in their new street cars, they would ignore the advice of the rangers to park at the lower level and pack in their gear, and try to make it on four wheels. Except for a cleanup crew who patrolled the roads every few days, some of the trails would soon have resembled junkyards, having become a graveyard of abandoned mufflers.

On one such trail, a long blue Cadillac was clawing its way up the steep slope, lurching from one rut to the next, bottoming out with sickening crashes of metal against rock and hard-packed earth. On its gleaming imitation leather top, a huge green plastic baggage carrier strained at the tightly stretched shock cords that held it to the luggage rack. These cords, gaily striped with metal hooks at each end, had been intended to lash down loads on a motorcycle rack or to attach a suitcase to the trunk of a sports car. Lashed around the big baggage carrier, they were strained to their utmost endurance.

Inside the Cadillac, a heavy-set man clutched the wheel and mashed his foot to the floor. He was afraid to lose momentum. Once stopped, he would spin out trying to move the car again, and there wasn't room to turn around. Nor could he back down that winding trail. He was committed.

But, he thought, as he smashed over another hump in the road, the Caddie would never be the same again.

'Hang on!' he shouted, as the car reached what looked like the crest of a hill.

The twelve-year-old boy beside him had been hanging on for quite a while now. He was afraid they were going to crash into a tree.

The road widened as they topped the grade, and his father hit the brake to keep from passing the camp site. As usual, he forgot that the Caddie had power brakes, and its nose dipped and slammed into the ground, and he and his son were thrown forward into the dashboard.

'Goddamn it!' yelled the man, glaring at the boy as if it were his fault. 'Lousy power brakes!'

He turned into the camp area. As he pulled up onto the sod, the car bounced up and down as if it were mounted on a pogo stick.

They got out. The man walked around the car, inspecting it. There were enough dents to make him grit his teeth, but the big blue Caddie was apparently unharmed otherwise.

He pushed down on the hood and let go.

The car tried to become a yo-yo. It leaped up and down as if alive.

'Stinking shocks are gone,' mumbled the man. He glared at his son. 'Well, Fred, how about it? Are you waiting for the sun to go down? Get that luggage rack untied.'

The boy climbed up onto the hood and began to struggle with the shock cords. They were drawn too tight for his twelve-year-old fingers to pry free.

'Come *on!*' yelled his father.

'They won't come loose,' called the boy. 'They're too tight.'

'Oh, hell,' said the man. 'Get down. I have to do everything myself. I don't know why I take you camping, anyway.'

The boy, sliding down the hood, didn't know why either. Because it always turned out like this, with his father shouting at him for not being able to correct for some mistake in planning that the man himself had made.

The camp grounds in the parks are filled with such misplaced vacationers. With no aptitude for adjusting to the woods, they try to force the woods to adapt to them. The result is always a miserable visit.

'You've got to use a little muscle,' said the man. He slipped one of the shock cords loose, and once free it whipped out of his hands, taking off a little skin in the process, and slashed the metal tip against the side of the car, just behind one of the fancy opera windows.

The man saw paint fly and said, 'Oh, my God!' The car was less than two months old, and it looked as if this single trip had already depreciated it by a couple of thousand dollars. He slid down from the open door, where he'd been standing, and examined the damage.

The scratch was enormous, and had gone through paint and primer to bare metal, which was dented with a long, narrow mark that would have to be filled.

'Now look,' he told the boy. 'Why do you make me nervous? If you didn't make me nervous, this wouldn't have happened. But you always make me nervous.'

Frightened, the boy said, 'I'll unzip the carrier.' He wanted to be out of reach. After outbursts like this, furious slaps usually followed.

'Sure you will,' his father said sarcastically. 'And you'll rip it, right? That's all we need after everything else. A scratched car and a ripped zipper.'

'I'm good at zippers,' said the boy. 'I can do it. I always fix Mom's zipper when it gets stuck.'

'Some trick,' mumbled the man. He wondered where he'd put the bourbon. A drink would go down good right now.

A green ranger vehicle came down the hill and turned into the clearing. The man did not hear it coming, and almost fell over the trunk of his car when he suddenly saw it. His attitude changed instantly. He was eager to please, to ingratiate himself with Authority, lest he be arrested for breathing.

To Kelly Gordon, leaning out the Toyota's window, he said, 'Hello, Officer. How do.'

Kelly bit his lip to keep from grinning. He had seen many like this man—cowed and respectful in the presence of a uniform, loud-mouthed and resentful of its authority once it was gone.

Kelly said, 'I'd like a word with you.'

The man approached the ranger vehicle, wiping sudden sweat from his forehead. 'Why, sure.' He looked at the Cadillac. 'I . . . I'm parked all right, I think. What—'

Feeling pity, Kelly said, 'Hey, mister, settle down. You haven't done anything wrong.'

Disbelievingly, the man said, 'I haven't?'

'You're just fine. I only wanted to tell you to be careful, don't wander off up toward the high country.'

'Careful?' The man's voice rose. 'Why should we be careful?'

'We had a little trouble with a bear and—'

The man went pale. 'Bears? Oh, my God!'

His son said happily, 'I like bears.'

The man yelled at him, 'But we don't feed them. It's against the law, right?' This last was to Kelly. 'We always obey the law.'

'You see any bears, stay well away from them,' Kelly said. 'We think one attacked some campers yesterday up in area R-Four.'

'Attacked?' The man was trembling visibly.

'It doesn't happen often,' said the ranger.

'What—were they—'

Kelly didn't want to say it, but he had to give this man all the facts. 'They were killed. But—'

'My God,' the man repeated. 'Killed? Freddie, did you hear that? You and your bears you like so much. What are you doing up there on top of the car? Get down right now. We're getting out of here.'

Kelly, not wanting their vacation to be ruined, said, 'I don't think there's really anything for you to worry about down here. Just obey a few basic rules. Stay out of the high country, and—'

'Sure,' said the man, anger rising in his voice. 'Stay in our car all day. No, sir. Not me. Come on, Freddie. Get that damned thing zipped up again. We're going home.'

Kelly said, 'Mister, there's no reason to panic. You're in Area Two, and there's every reason to believe you're safe here. Bears usually stay up in the high country. That's where the . . . accident took place yesterday. We're just taking a few precautions—'

'Fine,' the man almost yelled. 'And that's what I'm doing, too. Taking precautions. We're taking the precaution of getting the hell out of here.'

Kelly shrugged. 'There's no reason to, but if you want, that's your right. Turn in your sticker at the gate, so somebody else can get the camp site.'

'How about a refund?' the man asked.

Kelly gave him a tight smile and drove away. As soon as the green Toyota was out of sight, the man raised his voice, 'Power crazy, bossing people around. I've seen his sort before.' He looked up at the boy, struggling with the zipper.

'What's taking you so long?'

Fred said, his voice frightened, 'I think it's stuck, Daddy.'

'Sure,' said his father. 'I thought you knew everything about zippers. Well, there's a trick to it.' He climbed up and took over. 'Let me show you. You hold the edges straight. Tighter. I'll pull.'

The boy pulled the fabric as tight as he could. 'Okay,' he said.

'Got it?' demanded his father.

'Yes. But—'

'Now what?'

'I don't think you'd better jerk it, Daddy. It goes better if you do it slowly.'

'Slowly is how you catch the fabric with the teeth. Fast is how you close a zipper. You just watch me.'

He gave one rapid motion with all his strength, and with an awful tearing sound the whole zipper ripped loose.

Furiously, the man hurled the zipper down to the ground and yelled, 'Now look what you made me do!'

The boy shrank back against the windshield. He knew what was coming.

Tom Cooper came down the steep slope carefully. It had been a harder climb up to Powder Ridge than he'd anticipated. He was hot, and he was tired. He envied Gail.

She was gone from the stream where he'd left her. But he saw her tracks going upstream. He smiled. He knew all about the waterfall, and the beauty of the glade.

He called, 'Gail?'

She didn't answer. Slowly, he traced his way up along the stream's edge.

The water was cloudy today. Almost reddish.

He came around the boulder and found her clothing and the rifle there. He smiled. This was too good to be true. He looked around. She was nowhere in sight.

She'd known he would be back soon. If this wasn't an invitation, it would serve.

There was only one place she could be, he realized. Hiding under the waterfall. He'd taken more than one co-ed visitor there during the past summer.

He slipped out of his boots and rolled up his pants. He knew how to get past the curtain of water without getting wet. Carefully, he picked his way through the sharp underwater stones.

A shimmering glaze of crimson slid past his ankles. He was looking at the waterfall, and didn't notice it.

Just before he reached the falls, something nudged his leg, and this time he looked down.

It was a red chunk of meat, torn from the body of some living creature.

A stab of fear struck Tom's heart cold. He felt a wave of dizziness stagger him.

He saw what his eyes perceived, but his mind would not accept it for one long, terrible moment.

The chunk of meat had *fingers*.

Tom screamed. He might have been calling, 'Gail!' or it might have been only a mindless roar of fear and anger. He plunged into the waterfall, heedless of getting drenched, and disappeared behind its cascading facade.

There was a long pause, and then—from under the falls—came a cry of such rending pain and sadness that a nearby squirrel, feeding on fallen nuts, turned and ran up the tree.

The music from the juke box in the Wildhorse Mountain Lodge bar was sprightly, but the atmosphere in the rest of the bar was one of dark gloom.

Walter Corwin worked behind the bar, mixing drinks for the overflow crowd of visitors who had come down from the camp sites. His rooms were full, unusual for this time of year. But rather than cut their vacations short, many campers had decided to spend the extra money for a room at the lodge.

He should have been elated at this good fortune. But Corwin was gloomy too. Allison had not volunteered details about the two campers who had been killed in the high country, but without seeking, the details came to him through overheard conversations at the bar.

And now that cute little girl who had filled the ranger uniform so well. It made him sick.

In the corner, Kelly Gordon sat with Allison. His highball glass was empty, and he was popping ice cubes into his mouth and crunching them.

Allison said, 'Have another drink. The house is buying.'

He shook his head slowly.

'It'd do you good,' she urged.

'I sent her up there,' he said. 'Jesus, when will I stop remembering?'

'With luck, twenty-five years. But probably never. Don't try, Kelly. There's no way you're going to drown her out. Accept the pain, live with it. And don't blame yourself. She was a ranger doing a job. It could just as easily have been Tom.'

The pain showed on his face. 'That poor bastard. He found her.'

Allison said, 'They had a thing, didn't they?'

Kelly shrugged. 'Could be. If they didn't already, they were going to. It was in the cards.'

'Is anybody with him?'

'Don Stober. I think they're getting drunk.'

'Not such a bad idea,' she said.

He started to get up. 'I ought to be up there right now with a goddamned elephant gun.'

She pulled him back down. 'No you shouldn't. Didn't you tell me once that you never intended to kill anything again?'

'Total recall, that's what you've got.'

'I don't like killing either,' she said.

'Maybe I'm not cut out for this job,' he said. 'I'm not a hunter any more. I give lectures at campfires. I'm a whiz at projecting nature slides, and when somebody needs a guide to take them through the woods looking at birds and butterflies, old Kelly's always available.'

'Hush up. For an ex-mercenary, you're doing just fine.'

'Allie,' he said, gripping the glass with both hands, 'I'm scared. There's a goddamned killer bear out there, and here I sit crushing ice cubes in my mouth. And where the hell is Scottie?'

'He'll get here,' she said. 'It's dark outside. There's nothing else you can do but wait.'

'I bet there is,' he said, squeezing his eyes tightly shut. 'The only trouble is, I'm too paralyzed with inertia to figure out what.'

'You're too hard on yourself.'

'It's like those years when I was married, and didn't like

being married, and didn't know how to go about getting *un*married.' He looked up at her. 'So I just stopped being a man for a while. You know what I mean.'

'No,' she said. 'I don't know what you mean.'

'I mean that I'm angry, and can't do anything about it. And I'm frightened, and can't do anything about that, either.'

'What you are,' she said, 'is tired and frazzled, and what you need is another drink to chase those goblins out of your head.'

'No,' he said. 'Booze won't do it.'

'Then how about another ice cube?' She took some ice from her glass and put it into his. He picked up one of the cubes and munched on it.

She watched him chew, and her heart ached at his misery. But there wasn't anything else she could say.

CHAPTER EIGHT

The helicopter made its egg-beater sounds over the edge of the clearing just below the timber line. It was cold in the chopper, because both doors had been left off this morning.

Kelly glassed the forest below with ten-power wide-angle binoculars.

Don Stober, at the controls, said, 'Maybe he's holed up in a favorite cave.'

Kelly shook his head. 'No. The reason we can't find him is because he's moving all the time. And he's got a million acres to cover his tracks.'

'Well, he can't stay under cover forever. If he comes near one of these clearings, we ought to pick him up.'

'How about putting this whirlybird down closer to the trees?'

'Negative. There's too much convection today. The thermals are popping off those rocks, and where there's updrafts, you find downdrafts too. I don't want to start chopping trees with those blades.'

Kelly lowered the binoculars. He blinked. 'I feel like those things have become part of my face.'

'How about patterns?' Don asked. 'Most bears get into some kind of routine.'

'The only patterns we know are that he likes to kill women, and he's always on the move.'

Don chuckled. 'Sort of like me. Always on the move, searching out poontang.'

Unamused, Kelly said, 'Yeah.'

'Which reminds me, where's that filly you've been riding?'

Kelly whipped his head around, and Don saw the anger in his eyes. He hurried to say, 'No offense, Kell. Just funning.'

'Some fun,' Kelly said. Then he stiffened. 'Hey, I see something. Take her down.'

Don tilted the yoke and the chopper began to lose altitude. Kelly pointed.

'See? Moving through those pines?'

Don nodded. He saw the dark figure clearly. 'That's our baby,' he said. 'He's a big one.'

Kelly reached for the dual set of controls. 'I'll fly her. You take the rifle.'

Don stared at him.

'Hurry up, damn it!' Kelly said. 'The S.O.B. sees us.'

'Don't you want to take him?'

'Put those crosshairs on him,' Kelly ordered. 'Move!'

Don shrugged and shoved the heavy rifle out, resting it against the edge of the hatch.

He searched for the dark object with both eyes, and then let the crosshairs of the telescopic sight snap into focus. His finger stroked the trigger.

'Wait until we're sure,' Kelly warned.

Suddenly the figure ran out into the clearing, waving its arms.

Don pulled the rifle back into the chopper. 'It's a man,' he said.

'Son of a bitch,' said Kelly, angrily. 'It's Scottie.'

'I've got her,' Don said, retrieving the controls.

'Let's go down,' Kelly said.

'Hang on,' said the other ranger.

The Hughes tilted and fought the wind and downdrafts, until it made a shaky landing near the man below.

Arthur Scott came over and leaned against the helicopter, the blades winding down above him.

'Are you guys crazy?' he asked. 'Damn it, I saw a rifle pointed at me.'

'Scottie, you were supposed to meet me down at the station,' Kelly said. 'What the hell are you doing up here?'

'It dawned on me that it was pretty silly to come all the way down and turn right around and come up again. So I stayed here and started looking for your bear. I radioed a message through Barney.'

'I didn't get it,' Kelly said. 'What I did get was another

reaming out by Kittredge. He wants some action.'

'Well, for openers,' said the naturalist, 'you can inform him that the bear isn't one of ours.'

'How sure are you?'

'Positive.'

'You still should have come down. Kittredge likes to have a real roll call, see the troops all mustered up in a bunch.'

'Besides, which, old buddy,' said Don, 'you just now nearly got your tail shot off.'

Scott grinned. He was a big man, and when he smiled his face seemed to be all teeth. 'That would have been a shame,' he growled.

'Oh, you're a big bag of grits, I'll give you that,' Don went on. 'But what would you have done if you had caught up with that big black?'

'It's not a big black,' said Scott. 'It's a grizzly.'

Kelly said, 'Grizzly?'

Don said, 'Bull. There ain't no grizzlies up here. I've counted every bear in the woods. More than once. Not a grizzly among them.'

'They were killed off years ago for bounty,' said Kelly.

Scott said, 'Well, one of them survived.'

'How did we miss him?' asked Kelly.

'I don't know,' said the naturalist. 'But that's not all. This isn't your standard issue grizzly.'

'How so?' said Don.

'A normal grizzly goes seven, maybe eight feet tall.'

'Which is plenty tall enough for me,' said the ranger.

Scott said slowly, 'Well, this one is at least fifteen feet tall.'

They had begun loading Scott's gear into the helicopter. At this, Kelly stopped and said, 'That's impossible. They don't come that big even in Alaska.'

'He's been marking the trees,' Scott said. 'I measured them. His claw prints go up so high it's unbelievable. He's establishing his territory, and he won't be challenged on it. There's nothing taller in the woods.'

The rangers nodded. They were familiar with the normal bear's method of protecting his range. The claw marks, placed as high up a tree as a bear could reach, became bench marks against which each new invader would measure himself. If he could not scratch the tree higher, he turned around and looked for hunting grounds someplace else. If he beat the previous owner's height, either a battle ensued, or the first bear surrendered his territory and moved on.

'That's unreal,' Don said. 'Fifteen feet?'

'And weighing at least two thousand pounds,' Scott said, tossing his pack into the baggage compartment of the chopper.

'How do you know that?'

'The depth of his paw prints.'

Don Stober shook his head. 'You make him sound like some kind of prehistoric monster. I don't believe in science fiction.'

'Neither do I,' said Scott. 'At least, not the fiction part. But I have a hearty respect for science, and my expensive education reminds me that at one time there were grizzlies that large. The books call them *Arctodus-Ursus Horribulus*. They were one of the mightiest carnivore during the Pleistocene era.'

Kelly, listening impatiently, said, 'And when was that?'

'Around a million years ago,' said the naturalist.

'And what are you suggesting? That one of those million-year-old babies managed to survive? How? Frozen in a glacier, like that mammoth the Russians thawed out in Siberia?'

'No. But he must have had hearty ancestors with really enduring genes. He was probably born of normal grizzly parents, but he's a throwback to the Pleistocene period. He'd be an outsider to even his own pack, that large. They probably drove him out, or he drove them away.'

'How come we never saw him before?' asked Don. 'We couldn't have missed something that big.'

The naturalist pointed up toward the crest of the mountain. 'My guess is he was on the other side, on that private land where nobody ever went. Until the shale oil boys arrived, that is.'

'And they chased him over here?' asked Kelly.

'It's the most logical theory,' said Scott. 'One more thing to blame on the Arabs.'

'Well, what's a million-year-old bear doing over here anyway?' demanded Don Stober.

'Looking for something to eat,' said the naturalist. 'Most bears are omnivores. Especially grizzlies. It'd be easier to make a list of what they won't eat than what they will. They live for their bellies. But something, maybe his size, has turned this one into a carnivore. The son of a bitch simply loves meat.'

He almost said the rest, but it wasn't necessary.

Human meat.

As they rode down to the ranger station in the Hughes chopper, Kelly Gordon realized that his worst fears had come true.

Any rogue bear was bad enough. But a grizzly standing fifteen feet tall was nightmarish.

Kelly had known, deep down, that a bear was responsible. But he hoped that the evidence would prove otherwise. Now, Scott's discovery of the bear sign—and especially the fact that it was a grizzly—would start events in motion that might eventually destroy all he and the other rangers had been working to achieve.

Bear cubs are blind and completely helpless at birth, during the chill of winter when the mother is hibernating. But the cubs feed from the teat until spring, and usually come out of the cave weighing thirty pounds or more, frisky, and ready for play.

The giant grizzly who had come over the mountain was huge when he emerged from his birth cave. While mother bears and their cubs usually enjoyed a summer of happy play together, the mother lying in a cool stream with the cubs, teaching them to fish, cuffing them when they became too energetic, the big grizzly had not had such loving times.

Before July, he was as big as his mother, and frightened her. One night, she simply vanished, leaving him to fend for himself. This was unusual, for most mother grizzlies will die defending her cubs. And the usual training period for a cub is two years at his mother's side.

But the big bear survived. And he staked out his territory with instinct ruling him. If he was slower to learn, with no teacher, he was also bigger and stronger than anything else in the forest, and that gave him the extra edge he needed to live. Twice, foolish packs of wolves tried to drag him down, and several died for their error.

Because of the high elevation at which he lived, the big grizzly had never been seen by man. If he had, the stories would probably have been dismissed as outright lies. Even scientists admit that not more than fifty percent of bear stories are true.

Although a throwback, the giant bear earned his name of grizzly because his fur, multi-colored with silver, gray, yellow and deep brown, gave him the grizzly appearance of an old man's beard.

The Indians called the grizzly bears 'Moose Killer,' because only a grizzly could bring down those bovine elephants of the forest. The giant bear had never been seen by an Indian, but if he had, another legend would have been born.

Like most grizzlies, he was powerfully built, with a great hump above his shoulders that marked him apart from even the tallest black bear, the *Ursus americana*, which is the only other bear indigenous to the North American continent..

Able to run almost as fast as a horse, the normal grizzly often startles those who come upon him in the forest by streaking away with a sprightliness that astonishes those who think of bears as clumsy and bumbling.

Like the shark, the grizzly has been designed as an efficient eating machine. His teeth are canine, and the giant elastic muscles that power his jaws are able to crunch his molars through a deer's leg and bone like a knife through soft cheese.

But the grizzly's most terrible weapons are his forepaws. Ending in razor-sharp claws that may be six inches long, capable of severing a victim's head with one powerful blow. Like man's feet, the grizzly's are plantigrade, with heels, and toes that are tipped with the fearful claws.

Although he hears nearly as well as a man, the grizzly's eyes are poor. Scent is his chief sense, and he uses it to spot his prey. It is this well-developed sense of odor that keeps him out of man's way most of the time, for the average grizzly wants nothing to do with the two-legged predator.

But the beast that came over the mountain was not an average grizzly, not in size, and not in instinct. For he had now tasted the red meat of an easy kill, and had also developed a growing hatred for those he killed, and until he himself was brought down, he would continue to kill both for food and for vicious sport.

Camp site A-2, near the blue lake, had full hookups for campers and RVs, and it was still nearly filled. The rangers had assured the visitors that the bear was in the high country, and besides, what bear in his right mind would wander into what looked like a supermarket parking lot, filled with vehicles, noisy radios and TV sets crackling with the latest exploits of the FBI?

Several of the campers near the road had gathered wood (dead falls were permitted, but no cutting) and built a cheery fire in a stone-ringed pit provided by the park engineers. The popping of beer tabs and the occasional clink of a bourbon bottle made the evening merrier.

Two young boys, perhaps seven years old, stalked each other around the wood pile. One carried a toy machine gun.

'You're the bear,' he yelled. 'I got you. Bang-bang-bang!'

The other boy, the 'bear,' clutched his chest and died.

'Tommy!' called a shrill female voice. 'You get out of that dirt and right over here!'

The 'bear' got up and ran over to his mother, who gave him a sharp slap. 'You go inside and wake up your daddy. It's time to eat.'

Near the fire, Sally and Harry Dunham sat in the shadows. They were so close together that it was hard to tell where Sally ended and Harry began. His exploring hand completed the joining.

'You're up to no good,' she whispered.

In the best W. C. Fields imitation, Harry said, 'Just fondling the merchandise, m'dear.'

Sally did a fair version of Mae West. It was their little game before love. She said, huskily, 'I'd say you've got something more in mind than squeezing the tomatoes.'

'Sointenly do, m'dear,' he drawled.

She stirred. 'In that case, let me throw on something more . . . comfortable. And why don't y'come up and see me sometime?'

'*Dee*lighted,' he growled, flicking an imaginary cigar.

She strolled over toward their Dodge pop-up camper, parked at the edge of the camp site where there was privacy and plenty of shade during the day from the tall pines which surrounded the site.

Deliberately, she switched her ample behind at Harry, knowing that it drove him wild. In four years of marriage, he had never tired of admiring her plump derriere.

As she clicked the flimsy door shut, she thought she heard him growl tantalizingly behind her.

She smiled and plugged in an eight-track tape of Ravel's Bolero. Harry simply went ape screwing to Bolero. It was her signal to him to give her two minutes to strip, and then come in ready for action.

Tonight she'd wear the dark blue peignoir. Harry liked pulling it up slowly. From the rear, of course.

At the fire, Harry heard the first pulsating sounds of the music. He felt the urge beginning to stir, and shifted his position slightly. No need to let the other campers at the fire see what he was thinking about.

He looked at his watch, gave a great yawn. 'Well,' he said, 'Time to turn in.'

'Yeah,' chuckled a young man nearby, seated with his girlfriend. 'It's really late. Almost six o'clock.'

Harry stretched, his back to the fire.

Mama, he thought, I'm *ready*!

Then there was an explosion of movement from the camper. It shook violently, and he heard the canvas top ripping like the sound of a low-flying jet.

He started to move toward it, but the world was in slow motion. He thought he saw a giant shape reaching down into the top of the Dodge, and he shouted, 'Sally! Look out!'

She never heard him. The huge claws had dug deep into her stomach and she was making soundless, gasping motions of her mouth, the kind seen when a fish dies on the beach. The pain was so intense that all she could do was gurgle, deep in her throat, and plead in her mind for it to stop.

The group around the fire had leaped up and were frozen in fear. They saw a giant, shadowy thing behind the camper, but no one recognized what it was. Then there was a flash of white, as Sally was dragged through the camper's torn roof, and someone cried, 'Jesus, that's a woman!'

Harry made a wordless sound in his throat and tried to run toward the camper. Two men nearby caught his arms and held him back.

Now Sally found her voice. 'Oh, no, God!' she screamed. 'Not me, not me! No, God, no!'

The voice was cut off as her body smashed against a tree trunk. The creature had her by the feet and beat her back and forth from tree trunk to tree trunk, and after the second impact the woman stopped screaming.

But Harry didn't. Inside his head, he never would.

Incredibly, Avery Kittredge arrived at the camp site before Kelly. He was waiting, in his neatly ironed green uniform, a shiny Colt .38 strapped around his waist.

He looked at his watch. 'So you finally got here,' he told Kelly.

Kelly nodded. 'I guess you heard the radio report.'

'That's my job,' Kittredge said, loud enough for the shocked campers to overhear. 'Is the ambulance with you?'

'Coming up the road now.'

Harry Dunham sat on a log near the smouldering remains of the fire. One man was trying to get him to take a drink. Harry kept pushing it away.

'Look at that camper, Gordon,' Kittredge said. 'He tore it open like an egg shell. I thought you claimed your bears were all up in the high country.'

'Not now, damn it,' Kelly said. He went over to the numbed man on the log. He helped him up. 'Come on, it's all right. My driver'll take you down to the hospital. We'll take care of everything up here. Come along.'

Like a child, Harry Dunham allowed himself to be led to the ranger vehicle. As he was helped in, he looked back and, in a small voice said, 'Would somebody please turn off my tape player?'

When Kelly's Toyota drove down the hill, it was passed by a battered jeep driven by Arthur Scott.

As the ambulance attendants went about their gory task, Scott, Kelly and Kittredge went off to one side of the clearing.

'We've been trying to reach you, Avery,' said Scott. 'I—'

'Let me talk first,' said Kittredge. 'Kelly, what the hell happened? You assured me these lower districts would be safe.'

'We thought they would be. But he came down. Maybe because our search parties spooked him.'

Kittredge drew himself up to his full five feet nine. 'Kelly, I've had it with you. This is your baby, your responsibility. I wash my hands of it.'

Kelly said, disbelievingly, 'You wash your hands? How the hell can you do that? This is your park, Mr. Supervisor.'

'And this is your district, nobody else's. And that god-damned bear is yours, too.'

'*Mr.* Kittredge,' said Arthur Scott, 'let me give you a few facts. You would have had them earlier, but you were off talking to the nice ladies about our noble park program.'

'This is none of your business, Scott,' said Kittredge. 'Kelly didn't do the job with those bears. That's the long and the short of it.'

'Don't try to be more of an asshole than you are,' Scott said gently.

Kittredge began to splutter.

Scott went on, 'I don't work for you, like Kelly, so don't think I won't go on television and spill the beans if you keep dodging the reality and the responsibility here. We've been trying to tell you, we've got a killer grizzly on our hands.'

The supervisor whirled on him. 'You're under my supervision, Scott, and don't you forget it. You're a maniac . . . always were. Running around bundled up in deer skins. There hasn't been a grizzly in these mountains for thirty years.'

'There is now,' said Kelly. 'Come on, Scotty, let's get the hell out of here. There's nothing to do tonight.'

'I'm not finished,' Kittredge said.

'Oh?' the ranger shot back. 'Maybe you want me to take a flashlight and track him out there in the dark?'

'Get me that goddamned bear,' Kittredge ordered, 'and get him fast.'

'We're trying,' Kelly said. 'Maybe if you could get us more men. That's one thing you're good at, talking to Washington.'

'And blow this thing further out of proportion? Are you mad? There's nothing unusual about a bear getting out of line every now and then. What's unusual is that your men can't seem to get on the ball and catch this one.'

Dr. Samuel Hallit, who had finished examining what was left of Sally Dunham, had joined them. He tried to make peace. 'Avery's right, Kelly. It used to happen a lot more often back in the old days, when the campers fed the bears, or left food around in the open to attract them. Not to mention the garbage patrol, luring bears down so the tourists could photograph them.'

'Mr. Kittredge,' said Scott. 'Do you take Stupid Pills? Why won't you accept that this is no ordinary bear?'

'That remark will go in your file,' snapped the Supervisor.

'Sure, we used to have bear accidents,' said Kelly. 'But

they didn't eat their victims. This one does. And like Scotty said—'

Dr. Hallit said, 'Gentlemen, four people have been killed. Something has to be done, and arguing about who's responsible isn't going to help.'

Kittredge said, 'You've got more than enough men to handle this, Kelly. I warn you, if you don't do the job, I will.'

He turned and stalked off without giving time for an answer.

Kelly gave a low whistle.

'Hold that expression,' said a female voice. It was Allison. She clicked off two exposures, almost shoving the camera lens into Kelly's ear.

'Come on, Allie,' he said. 'No games.'

'What games? I'm getting some terrific shots.'

Grimly, he said, 'Including what was left of that poor woman?'

'You bet,' she said. 'I shot two rolls of high-speed color, and then I went out in the woods and threw up.'

CHAPTER NINE

No war is without its respites, its quiet moments for reflection and renewal, and the war against the mountain beast was no exception.

Having sent his Toyota down the mountain, Kelly accepted a ride from Allison, and that led to an offer of a drink—in her cabin, since the bar was crowded—and there was a warm and cheerful fire, and more than one drink, and . . .

Kelly added a log to the glowing embers of the fire which had burned down to the last red coals. The room was dimly lit, with only one shaded lamp on. The radio played quiet music, a waltz by Mantovani.

He'd slipped back into his jeans, but above the waist he was bare, and the perspiration was still drying, gleaming on his heavily muscled shoulders.

Near him, stretched out on the big black bearskin rug, Allison stirred under the light blanket. She made contented noises.

'Just fixing the fire,' Kelly said. 'Go back to sleep.'

'Who's sleeping?' she mumbled.

He sipped at a wine glass half filled with brandy, and stirred the fire, which was blazing up again.

'Share the wealth,' Allison said.

'Are you referring to the brandy?'

'What else would I be asking for?'

He smiled in memory of the past hours. 'A guy never knows.'

He moved closer to her. The blanket was just above the twin mounds of her breasts. Then, as she moved, it slipped down.

Kelly let a few drops of the brandy spill onto her skin, all rosy in the firelight. Then he bent down and kissed the brandy away. Allison writhed and whispered, 'That tickles. But don't stop.'

'I wouldn't have stopped before. But you fell asleep.'

'Look who's talking. You were snoring five minutes after we—'

She stopped. It wasn't necessary to use the words. His hand stroked her.

He held the glass to her lips, and she sipped.

He said, 'It was good. I'd forgotten how good it could be.'

'You?' She laughed. 'I've heard about your exploits.'

'Yeah,' he said, 'and that's all they were. A few sweaty minutes without meaning and without love.'

'I didn't know you were acquainted with that word,' she said softly.

'What word?'

'The four letter one that can be either the most wonderful thing a person can say . . . or the most damnable lie ever heard.'

'Love?'

'See, you do know how to say it.'

'Do you?'

She reached up and drew him down. The blanket had fallen off all the way now. She kissed him, slowly and deeply.

Moments passed. When he drew back, he said, 'Where did you learn to do that?'

'With the tongue?'

'Among other things.'

'I had a liberal education,' she said. 'I used to practice for this moment, siphoning gas out of parked cars.'

He finished the brandy. 'You're crazy,' he said, making the words a caress.

'And you're a chameleon.'

'How so?'

She traced her finger along his strong bones. 'Your jaw. Changes. Always changes. It's different in each new light.'

'You should know,' he said, lifting an imaginary camera. 'Click!'

She covered her breasts with simulated modesty. 'Oh, sir, please. Give me the negatives. I'll pay anything for them.'

He leered. '*Any*thing.'

She lowered her eyes. 'Yes . . . even that.'

They laughed together gently, and the fire painted golden patterns on their bodies.

He kicked off his jeans and slipped under the blanket with her.

'Wait a minute,' she said, pushing him away. 'Before this goes any further, I've got to know something.'

'Shoot,' he said, cupping his hands around her.

'What's your sign?'

'My what?'

'Your astrological sign.'

He nuzzled her shoulder and bit gently. 'You're kidding.'

'No, I'm not.'

'All right. I'm a Taurus.'

She shoved him away. 'Oh, hell!'

'What's the matter?'

Trying to contain her laughter, and failing, she choked, 'I'm a Leo. The book says we're not compatible.'

As he pulled her to him for the complete embrace they had both been working up to, Kelly said, 'You know what you can do with your book.'

There had not been a legal hunt in the park for more than thirty years. At one time, hunters drawn by lot were allowed to harvest the excess deer, but that practice was stopped before the Second World War, and had never been resumed.

Now trained sharpshooters were brought in whenever the herds had outgrown their grazing range, and the meat was donated to the state hospital.

But the convoy of jeeps, pickup trucks and other off-road vehicles that lined up outside the park's main gate early this morning was filled with anything but sharpshooters. They were a motley bunch, some in camouflage green, some wearing hunters' flame orange, one actually dressed in a rumpled business suit. The only thing they had in common were the rifles they carried.

The gate ranger had received instructions to let the hunters come in. But as he watched them drive past, in the dull gray of dawn, he shook his head.

He turned to his partner. 'Kelly's not going to like this,' he said.

'Some of those guys have got dogs,' said the other ranger. 'That's illegal.'

'The whole thing's illegal. But they're doing it, and we have to let them. Orders.'

One party of hunters stopped at the edge of the road, and they planned their routes.

A man driving a battered red Ford pickup leaned out and called to another hunter, who piloted an International Scout, 'Hey, Carl, did you bring those extra three-hundred express cartridges?'

'Got 'em right here,' said the other man.

Up the mountain, three rifle shots made a string of lonely *boom-boom-boom*'s which echoed down the valleys for fully half a minute.

Carl said, 'Damn it, somebody's already up there shooting.'

'They didn't get him, though,' said the other man. 'One shot, meat. Two shots, maybe meat. Three shots, no meat, That guy missed his first shot and just kept squeezing them off.'

Carl said, 'Let's get this show on the road. I want to get me a shot at that bastard.'

The hunters soon filled the woods. Men and dogs ran in all directions. The dogs were as mixed a bag as the hunters. Some were bird dogs, others were rabbit-trained beagles. One enterprising hunter had actually brought along his wife's poodle.

That nobody was shot by accident in that first hour was a minor miracle, because the nervous men fired at anything that moved.

By the time the sun came up, the mountain sounded as if a small war had broken out on its slopes.

One party paused, cold and tired. They hadn't brought an axe, but there was deadfall wood, and one man knocked down a wooden sign and used it to help start the fire.

The sign's legend read, NO HUNTING.

One man saw a black shadow moving in the underbrush, threw his 30-30 to his shoulder, and fired.

Something thrashed in the thicket, and went still.

Carefully, the hunter advanced.

He looked down at what he'd shot.

'Oh, hell,' he said.

He had killed someone's big Labrador retriever.

Don Stober said to Kelly, 'You're late.'

Embarrassed, Kelly said, 'I overslept. What the hell's going on?' He looked around the office. 'Where's Scottie?'

'He got an early start. He's out there tracking. I just hope some stupid hunter doesn't shoot him.'

Kelly listened to the distant shots. 'Hunters? What the hell are hunters doing in the woods?'

'Looking for our bear.'

'On whose authority? Who the hell opened the woods to hunters?'

'I'll give you one guess.'

Kelly swore. 'That goddamned Kittredge.'

'He passed the word around High City last night. I hear he authorized a five hundred dollar bounty.'

Kelly poured some coffee and drank it, holding the cup in shaking hands. Too much brandy, too much loving. . . .

'For God's sake,' he said. 'Has he gone bananas? They're more likely to kill one of the rangers than that bear.'

Don shrugged. 'Me, I've always thought most hunters are a little crazy. They might get lucky and find him.'

'Like hell,' said Kelly. 'Those bastards are shooting at everything that moves, including themselves. Listen to it up there. It sounds like the Battle of the Bulge.'

He slammed down the coffee, picked up the phone, and began dialing Avery Kittredge's private number.

Not all of the hunters on the mountain were gun-happy amateurs.

One man, Phillip Boyson, a fifty-one-year-old Texan, made his solitary way through the forest with care and planning. He searched for the bear's markings, and when he found the first set of claw marks, high on a tree, he looked up at them and gave a low whistle.

Boyson had hunted big game all over the country and in Canada and Alaska, too. He had stayed away from the mob scene that was being enacted in the easily accessible areas. He knew that the bear would steer clear of them too.

The bounty did not interest him. But the thought of being the first hunter to bag a grizzly in this state in the past fifty years did.

He moved quietly through the woods, following the almost invisible trail left by the bear. He saw occasional claw marks, and twice, piles of droppings left deliberately to stake out the animal's territory.

What he didn't see was the beast who was stalking him.

Kelly slammed down the phone.

'That pompous ass!' he yelled.

Don asked, 'What did he say?'

'He'll talk about it. But not here. We've got to go down to his office. He's too goddamned *busy* to come up here where the action is.'

'He's not dumb,' said Don Stober. 'He doesn't want to get a load of buckshot in his tail.'

The hunter found a torn patch of earth where the bear had rooted for wild onions. The dirt was still moist. The beast had been here not long ago.

Only now did Boyson chamber a shell into the breech of his rifle. He clicked off the safety. He was ready for anything.

But while he was tracking the bear, the bear was tracking *him*.

The grizzly was almost within reach of the hunter when Boyson caught a trace of the animal's distinctive odor. Most men would have ignored it, and they would have died. He knew better, and whirled, his rifle snapping up to his shoulder.

The move saved his life. The grizzly's great claw was already sweeping toward him. Instead of tearing flesh, it caught the wood stock of the rifle and hurled it from the man's hands as he squeezed the trigger. The sound of the shot was astonishingly loud in the stillness of the forest. It startled the bear, he drew back, and the hunter seized the opportunity to run as fast as he could.

He got a bare fifty yards head start, and the grizzly dropped to all fours and began to chase him. The huge animal gathered speed, and the hunter could hear its breath puffing with each giant stride.

Boyson reached the edge of a large stream. The grizzly was close behind him.

Desperately, the man threw himself into the swiftly flowing water. The bear hesitated. He did not fear water, but before he could act, the man had been carried downstream and out of sight around a bend.

The grizzly gave the equivalent of a shrug. There was plenty more food in the woods today. It wasn't necessary to exhaust himself chasing this one.

Although Avery Kittredge kept a nominal office in the park itself, he almost never visited it. He conducted his business from a handsome paneled room in the tallest building in High City, the Boulder Mining Center, a leftover from the boom days of the mid-thirties when silver had been taken out by the carload. Now the mines were closed, but all eyes were fixed on the oil shale operations over the mountain. If they proved out, that might mean new life for High City, which now existed more as base for the park activities and a tourist shopping center than anything else.

The 'Park Supervisor' sign on Kittredge's door was burned with a branding iron into a large chip of redwood. It always antagonized Kelly. There wasn't a redwood tree within a thousand miles of the park.

Kittredge, behind his huge, absolutely clean desk looked at Kelly and Don.

'Where's Scott?' he asked.

'Up on the mountain,' Kelly said shortly.

The two rangers were standing. It angered Kittredge.

'There are chairs in this office,' he said.

'I don't want to sit down,' Kelly said. 'I want some answers. What the hell are hunters doing up there in the park?'

'Sitting or standing, the answers you'll get are the same,' said Kittredge. He looked at the chairs and waited.

Don Stober decided to stop fighting city hall. He sat down. Kelly didn't.

'Last night I was in charge of this operation,' Kelly said. 'This morning I discover that I'm not. You went over my head.'

'I didn't have any choice,' Kittredge said. 'You weren't staying on top of the situation.'

'I had rangers in the field.'

'And who was supervising them? I called you last night around eleven. You were nowhere to be found.'

'My men don't need to be ramroded.'

'No? What did they come up with? I'll tell you. Diddly.'

'So you went right ahead and authorized that batch of maniacs. Why couldn't you wait to consult with me?'

'Because I'm tired of your pussyfooting around. It's almost as if you're on the bear's side instead of ours. The public wants action. So I gave it to them.'

Kelly sighed. 'And in the process you made it open season on every animal in the woods.'

'I gave clear instructions. The only target is bear.'

'Not bear. Grizzly. There's a difference.'

Kittredge shrugged. 'A bear is a bear. Just so we get him.'

'Wrong,' said Kelly. 'A bear is not a bear, believe it or

not. Listen, if we wanted to bring in hunters, it would have taken less than half a day to do it right, call for the professionals.'

'Every man up there has a valid license,' said Kittredge.

'Bull! What does that mean? That he's over sixteen and knows how to sign his name. Do you know what you've put up there in our woods? A bunch of roadhunters who do their best shooting over a beer down at Chauncey's. There's not more than two or three real hunters in that whole mob you saddled me with.'

Kittredge admitted, 'Sometimes you find one or two nuts, but we didn't have time to screen them out.'

'I want those amateurs out of my forest,' Kelly said.

Kittredge replied, 'It's not your forest, Kelly.'

'It's my jurisdiction, and I want them out, and right now.'

'I have authority to deny that request. Denied.'

'This is my district.'

'Your authority is granted by me,' said Kittredge. 'My concern is the welfare of the entire park, not just your section of it. In my judgment, this is the best way to handle the situation.'

'So it's okay for those nuts to go up there and shoot at anything that moves? Damn it, there are campers in those woods.'

'Not in R-Three and R-Four.'

'Do you think those so-called hunters are carrying around topographical maps? They wouldn't know it if they were on Mars.'

'Your campers are in no danger,' Kittredge said. 'Not if they stay where they're supposed to be.'

Kelly said, 'We've got a man-eating grizzly up there, and a bunch of silly-assed hunters who couldn't tell a bear from a beer keg, and you say my campers have nothing to worry about. That's the laugh of the year.'

'Are you through?' Kittredge asked coldly.

'Almost. I've got one more question.'

'Ask it.'

'Why have you always been after my ass? Ever since you took over, I've been on the griddle. I moved on this bear thing in the right way, and I followed the book. I should be getting good grades, not this crap.'

'The Service is changing,' said Kittredge. 'Maybe in the old days it was all right for a ranger to be a maverick like you. Not any more. We're a team effort. We don't have room for mavericks.'

'Without mavericks like me, you wouldn't have any forest. Your solid businessmen would have lumbered off every square acre. That forest isn't mine? You silly bastard, that forest is a part of me. What claim do *you* have on it?'

'I can bring charges against you for saying that,' Kittredge shouted.

'Great,' said Kelly. 'File them. Meanwhile, those stupid hunters you turned loose are in my jurisdiction, and I'm going to take care of them my way. If you think you can stop me, go ahead and try.'

He left.

Don Stober, who had been trying to stay out of the battle, got up.

'Nice seeing you again, Mr. Kittredge,' he said.

When Don and Kelly got to the Toyota, parked outside the Boulder Mining Center, they found Tom Cooper sitting in the back seat.

'Saw you parked here,' Tom said. 'Give me a lift?'

Kelly, starting the engine, said, 'You feel up to it?'

'I'm all right. Hung over. Yeah, I'm ready. Did you hear the news? One of those hunters saw our bear. Said he was twenty feet tall. Bear took his gun and everything. I know the guy. He's a good man in the woods. Take off five feet or so, and that's still a big mother up there.'

'Where is the hunter?'

'In the hospital. He had to swim down the rapids of Trout Creek to get away. But he's okay.'

'He was lucky,' Kelly said. 'The next one won't be. I'm going to get their asses down off that mountain.'

'Let them alone,' said Tom. 'Let them blow that bastard away. I wish I could.'

'Not this way,' said Kelly.

He put the vehicle in gear.

CHAPTER TEN

It was one thing for Kelly to decide to recall the hunters from the forest, and another thing to achieve it. The lazy ones, the road-hunters who drove around hoping to see something they might shoot from a car window, were easily found and told to go back to town. But in the forest's interior the more serious hunters were scattered all over the mountain, and finding them was no easy job. Kelly decided not to even try it. By getting out the majority of the hunters he had eliminated the most dangerous ones. He would handle the rest as he came upon them.

It was late afternoon by the time he had reorganized his forces. The hunter who had seen the bear had given him a good idea of where the grizzly was, and Kelly called down those rangers he could reach by radio and was forming a new hunting party.

He warned, 'Watch out for those birds Kittredge sent in. They'll shoot first and check to see if you have fur later.'

A CLICK! made him turn. Allison had just taken another photograph.

'When did you come up?' he asked.

'Few minutes ago.' They moved off to one side. She looked up at him. He peered around, realized that whatever they did was not going to go unnoticed, and leaned down to kiss her.

'Thanks,' she said. 'I know what a trauma that must have been for you, showing humanity in front of your troops. But I was feeling unloved.'

'Me too,' he said. 'I'm glad you came by.'

'Going hunting?' she asked.

'Yes. I think I know where he is. A hunter spotted him.'

'I'm coming with you,' she said, hitching up the strap of her gadget bag.

'No way,' he said.

'Now wait a minute—'

'Honey, it's a butcher shop out there, between our bear and those idiots shooting up the woods.'

'I can take care of myself.'

'No. I'd be thinking about you and worrying, when I should be watching out for the business we've got to do.'

'But, Kelly,' she said, trying to make him understand. 'This is my *book*. I've finally found my theme.'

'I'm sorry,' he said. 'Go ahead and hate me, but the answer is no.'

Tom Cooper joined them. 'We're all loaded,' he said.

'Okay,' said Kelly. 'Move them out.'

'I'll stay out of your way,' Allison said, almost pleading.

'No,' he repeated, firmly.

'Damn it, Kelly, I realize you've got your job to do. But I've got mine, too. I'm not playing games.'

'I know that, Allie. But this whole thing has gotten too dangerous. Find something else to photograph for your book.'

Angrily, she asked, 'Is that an order?'

'If you want it to be one.'

'From Kelly the Man, or Kelly the Ranger.'

'It's from both of us.' He reached for her. 'But Kelly the Man just doesn't want you to get hurt.'

'Well,' she said, pulling away, 'Kelly the Ranger can tell Kelly the Man to go straight to hell.'

She turned and walked away.

Night comes early in the mountains, and this first night of the big hunt settled down over the hazy valleys before six P.M.

One group of hunters, back-packing up the mountain, was clustered around a low fire. They were tired. It was one thing to sit on watch for a white-tailed deer, or a mule buck, but it was something else to scramble up one steep incline after another all day long.

The men lay in down-filled sleeping bags. They tossed, as aching muscles protested against the hard ground.

One awakened, sensing movement nearby.

He looked up—right into the open mouth of a bear.

He erupted from the sleeping bag with a piercing yell of fright. The other hunters thrashed, escaping from their own nylon cocoons.

The first hunter, who had grabbed his rifle as he fled, chambered a bullet. He threw up the rifle to fire.

Then, slowly, he lowered it and started to laugh.

A frisky bear cub pawed at the empty sleeping bag.

The hunter said, 'Boys, I just lost twenty years.'

Pat Clifford, a big, bluff man, lowered his own rifle. He said, 'Hey, this may be that grizzly's cub.'

The first hunter, Mike Newton, said, 'Naw. This is a black bear, not a grizzly.'

Pat persisted. 'You can't tell. He's kind of speckled. Look'.

A third hunter said, 'If he is, I'd suggest we throw his ass out in the woods. I don't want that bastard coming in here after any cub.'

'That's an idea,' Pat said. 'Listen, we can use the cub as bait. Tie him in the woods, wait until mama shows up and—' he made a shooting motion with his fingers. 'Blam.'

'That's not a bad idea,' Mike admitted. 'Who's got some rope?'

The original plan was to have someone on watch, waiting, but as the night wore on and tiredness ate away at their stamina, the hunters gradually filled up their sleeping bags again.

So when a huge claw reached out into the clearing and scooped up the bear cub, no one was awake to hear its pitiful whimpers of pain.

It took the headlights of the ranger vehicle, churning up the trail, to drag them back from slumber.

Kelly helped waken them by tooting the shrill horn. Again, they crawled out of their sleeping bags.

'Okay,' the ranger told them. 'The hunt's over for you boys. Pack up and move out.'

Pat Clifford argued, 'Listen, Kelly, you know us. We're steady. Let us help you.'

'How?'

Mike Newton said, 'We've got a bait staked out for that grizzly. A bear cub.'

'Where?'

'Over there—'

Mike stopped. The cub wasn't there any more.

They went over, and saw where the rope had been torn from the tree.

A few feet inside the trees, they found what was left of the cub.

Mike gagged. 'Oh, my God.'

'So you're steady, huh?' Kelly said with heavy sarcasm. 'Whose idea was it to use live bait?'

Pat said, shakily, 'Mine. But I—'

'Did anyone see what happened?'

Mike said, embarrassed, 'I was supposed to be on watch. But nothing was happening and—'

'You were all asleep,' said a new voice.

Arthur Scott, wearing buckskin, stepped out of the trees.

'Scottie,' said Kelly. 'Where the hell have you been?'

'Tracking our big friend. I think at one point I was only half an hour behind him. I came up on this camp shortly after he killed the cub. I've been waiting, to see if he'd come back.'

'Okay, fellows,' Kelly said. 'You heard me before. Start getting your gear together.'

'We found out one thing,' Scott said. 'Our grizzly is a male.'

Don said, 'How do you figure?'

'Only the males are cannibalistic. One of their favorite appetizers is a young cub.'

'Does knowing that help us?' Kelly asked.

'Maybe. Males travel alone, and they tend to repeat their routes. In other words, he may come back to the scene of the crime.'

'So he may be out there right now?'

'I'd bet on it,' said Scott.

Kelly turned to the five hunters. 'Change of plan. You guys game to help us flush him out?'

'I am,' said Pat. 'I can use that five hundred.'

'Me too,' said Mike. The rest of the hunters chimed in with their assents.

'You do it by the book,' Kelly said. 'My book. Nobody goes off on his own. And no sound shots. I don't want anything in these woods killed except that grizzly.'

'You're calling the shots, Kelly,' said Pat. 'How do you want us to go?'

'You guys get your tails up to the north ridge.'

'Pinto Pass?'

'Right. Form yourselves into a line, like a deer driving party. The rest of us will spread out and hold the line at Culver Basin. If he's between Pinto and here, that's where he'll be coming down.'

'You want us to bark?'

'Bark like dogs, beat tin pans, do anything you can to make that bastard turn and head down. He ought to come right at us.'

One of the hunters said, 'My dogs are down with my brother's party. Do I have time to get them?'

'Negative. You've got an hour and a half to get up to Pinto Pass, and start your drive.' He looked at his watch. 'That ought to give us some daylight.'

As the hunters began to gather their gear, Kelly went over to the Toyota.

'Tom, you get out here.'

Tom Cooper, incredulous, said, 'You're kidding. You're not going to cut me out of this now. No way. That bear's my baby!'

'I'm not cutting you out of anything. I want you to take watch from Arrow Tower. You ought to be able to get a shot if he comes down the east slope.'

'That's not my idea of hunting, sitting up in that old wooden firetrap. Let somebody else take it, I'll stay with the rest of you.'

Kelly said quietly, 'I know how much this means to you. Believe me, Tom, you've got the best chance of all of us of getting in a shot. We're going to be blocked by brush. You'll have a clear view. You're going to be our eyes and ears, with your radio. And maybe our firepower.'

Tom nodded. 'Okay. But I hope I don't miss it all.'

'If you see him, give us a shout. Channel nine.'

'Right,' said Tom. He gathered up his rifle and radio, and set off up the trail at a trot.

'We'll leave the wheels here,' said Kelly. 'Unload.'

Don started to hand him a rifle. Kelly waved it aside.

'Come on, Kell,' said Don. 'You aim to play Daniel Boone and wrestle with him?'

'You keep it,' said Kelly. 'You're a better shot than me anyway.'

Don stared at him, as the group of rangers packed up and moved out.

Arrow Tower was an old wooden structure that was nearly ready to fall down under its own weight and old age. It shook as Tom climbed the ladder leading to its porch. The tower had been built years ago as a temporary fire watch, and should have been torn down long ago. But it commanded a good view of the slopes coming down from Pinto Pass.

He took up position on the rickety porch and checked his rifle to be sure it was loaded. The safety was on, and he left it that way.

Tom pressed the transmit button on the radio. 'This is Cooper,' he said. 'I'm in position.'

'Ten-four,' said Kelly's voice. 'Keep us posted.'

The last hour of the night passed slowly. Kelly deployed his armed rangers along the basin, warning them not to smoke. A wild animal can detect cigarette smoke for miles.

There was no need to warn them not to doze; tension was so high that the breaking of a twig brought rifle barrels up.

Scott, near Kelly, said, 'Kelly, do we really have to kill him?'

'What choice do we have?'

The naturalist slipped what looked like a flare pistol out of his knapsack. 'This. Give me the first shot.'

'Why?'

'You don't understand. This is a rare find. Oh, I know he's killed, but there must be a reason. Kelly, there's a grizzly up there fifteen feet tall and weighing two or three thousand pounds. Let me try to capture him.'

Don Stober, on the other side of a low boulder, snorted. '*Capture* him? How? Draw down on him and say "hands up"?'

'Let Scottie finish,' said Kelly.

'This fires tranquilizer darts normally,' Scott said, holding out the odd-shaped pistol. 'But I've been experimenting with some new drugs.' He fished in his pocket and took out a long, pointed shell. 'These glass tips should penetrate his hide, and release the chemical agents into his bloodstream.'

Don examined the cartridge. 'Christ,' he said, 'this mama wouldn't even get through the hair on his chinny chin chin.'

Scott took back the shell and slipped it into his pistol.

'I want to study that bear,' he said. 'He's a genuine throwback to a million years ago.'

'Fine,' said Don. 'But first you have to knock him down, and I guarantee you, these BBs won't do it.'

'We'll see,' Scott said.

Kelly asked, 'How long after he's hit until the drugs put him down?'

'Ten seconds.'

'A bear his size can do a lot of damage in ten seconds.'

'I'll slip out in front,' Scott suggested. 'Then if the drugs don't work, you can still use the heavy artillery.'

'You slip out in front, Scottie,' said Don, 'and you're on the menu as his breakfast. By now I bet he's hungry again.'

'He just ate that cub,' said Kelly. 'Would he be hungry so soon?'

'I'm afraid he will,' Scott admitted. 'It takes a lot of food to sustain a two-thousand-pound animal. Particularly a bear. That may be why he's turned killer.'

'The cub was only the appetizer,' said Don. 'He's after bigger game. Listen, we used to have plenty of bear down Georgia way, and I've heard stories about them. Once they taste human meat, they won't settle for anything else.'

'That hasn't been proven,' Scott said. 'Man-killers usually have an injury, or illness. If it's cleared up, they revert back to normal behavior.'

'Is that what you have in mind for this baby?' Don asked. 'Rehabilitating him?'

'Why not, if it can be done? Isn't he worth saving?'

'Not in my book. I don't think it can be done, and even if it could, I wouldn't buy it for this bastard, not after what he did to Gail.'

'That's mere vengeance,' said the naturalist.

Don nodded. 'You bet your ass. And what's wrong with a little vengeance?'

'Punishing a wild creature is obscene. They can't reason. How can they be responsible for what they do?'

'Tell that to the tribe of Kiowa who were wiped out south of here.'

'What tribe?'

'Oh? Is there something about bears you don't know after all? Kelly, you heard the story, didn't you.'

Kelly nodded. 'I heard it. I don't know if it's true.'

'It's true all right,' said the other ranger. 'I read it in a book. Seems there was this big tribe of Kiowa, moving west. They camped on a river downstream from a town, and didn't know it was polluted. While the braves were out hunting, the rest of the tribe came down with the typhoid. They were all laid up. And just about then, a big pack of grizzlies smelled them out, strolled into the village, and ate 'em.'

'Ate them?'

'Each and every one, including the women, children and the sick old men. Just gobbled 'em up.'

'Fascinating,' Scott said.

'When the braves got back from their hunt, the bears were waiting, and they ate *them*, too. It was hell on wheels, Mr. Scott. For a couple of years, there was this big pack of grizzlies, roaming around, eating up Injuns.'

'Fascinating,' Scott repeated.

'Yeah,' said Don. 'Unless you happened to be an Indian.' He chuckled.

Scott realized he'd been had, and managed a smile in reward for the tall tale.

'Still,' he said to Kelly, 'I think I can root him out my way. I've got my skins with me. I can look like something wild and smell wild too. I can get close enough to hit him with the drugs.'

Don said, 'Scottie, can I have your mother's phone number? I better call her up, don't you think I'd better do that? I mean, does she know what you're doing, boy? Does she know she's got a forty-year-old certified fruitcake for a son, running around in animal skins and stinking like a dead-forty-days-ago fish?'

Shocked, Scott turned away.

'Shut it off,' Kelly said, angrily.

'Hey,' Don said. 'I was only kidding.'

Scott turned back to him. 'My mother's been dead for nine years,' he said. 'But if she were alive, I think she'd be happier with a certified fruitcake than if she had you for a relative, sonny.'

Don started to answer, but he was cut off by the sound of barking from up the mountain.

The bear drive had begun.

The sun was flirting with the edges of the mountains, but had not risen yet.

The air had that special chill that holds it still just before the day begins.

The original five hunters had been joined by another group, which also had three hunting dogs.

Now, in a skirmish line, they started down the mountain. The men shouted and barked. The dogs took up the baying too, and the noise was tremendous.

In the old tower, Tom heard them. He pressed the transmit button of his radio and said, 'Kelly, this is Tom. They're moving.'

'Roger,' said Kelly. He turned to Arthur Scott. 'Scottie, they've started the drive. If you see him first, he's yours. But I can't let you go up there alone.'

Scott's lips tightened. He made no answer, just took out the tranquilizer gun and checked the firing mechanism to be sure it was ready.

The beast was not startled by the barking. He had been aware of a disturbance in the natural rhythm of the forest for some hours now, and had made his way carefully along invisible trails to stay as far as possible from the intruders.

Despite his huge size, he moved quietly through the forest, keeping to the low areas where his bulk would not be silhouetted against the skyline.

He was hungry again. And somewhere ahead, he could smell the tantalizing odor of food.

Tom Cooper glassed the slope.

His radio made a tinny 'Beep.'

He picked it up. 'Cooper.'

'Kelly. See anything moving?'

'Just your mighty hunters. They're coming down the mountain like the charge of the light brigade.'

Kelly chuckled. 'Well, keep watching.'

'Ten-four,' said Tom. He lifted his glasses and continued his surveyal.

The beast knew food was nearby. He could smell it. But with his poor eyesight, he could not pinpoint its location.

The odor seemed to come from above....

Tom's radio beeped again.

He said into it, 'Yeah?'

'See anything?' Kelly asked.

'Just your hunters chopping up the woods.'

'Well keep looking. He's out there somewhere.'

Before Tom could answer, he felt the tower lurch. He grabbed for a handhold, looked down and saw the beast.

Kelly heard him shout, 'My God, it's the grizzly!'

'Where?'

But Tom was too busy to answer. The monstrous creature had hold of one of the tower's supporting legs, and was shaking it back and forth. It could not hold under such an assault for long.

He fumbled for the radio, but couldn't find it. He caught up his rifle, aimed it at the beast's throat, and fired.

The bullet hit. He heard the meaty slap it made as it tore into the grizzly. But the impact did not slow the beast's frenzied attack on the tower.

Slowly, like a falling tree, the tower toppled. As it did, Tom's rifle fired again, but this time the bullet went straight up into the rosy sky.

'Tom said something about the grizzly,' Kelly said. 'Let's get ready to move out.'

'I heard two shots,' Don said. 'They sounded like they came from the tower.'

Kelly handed the radio to a nearby ranger. 'You and Witham stay here on watch. We're going up there. Keep trying to reach Tom.'

The ranger did, and the fallen radio made intermittent beeping noises.

But no human heard them.

'Jesus H. Christ,' said Kelly, looking at the fallen tower. 'What happened here?'

Scott went forward, his quick movements out of place with his great size. He stepped over a fallen timber and looked down.

At his foot, half covered with torn earth, the radio went, 'Beep!'

And a few feet away, half-severed from his body, Tom Cooper's bloodied face stared up at a sunrise the young ranger would never see.

Scott turned away, nauseated and angry.

'Kelly,' he said quietly. 'The bear's been here.'

On the mountainside, a barrage of rifle shots rang out. Then, after a pause, two more—slowly, carefully fired. The kind of shots a hunter takes to finish off his fallen target.

The elated hunters dragged the bear into the clearing which surrounded the fallen tower.

Tom's body had been covered with a nylon ground cloth. The hunters did not even notice it.

Pat Clifford swaggered up to Kelly. 'Well,' he said, 'We got the bastard.'

Numbly, Kelly said, 'Where?'

'Up below the ridge.'

'Impossible. He's been down here. He wouldn't head back uphill.'

Pat said, proudly, 'Well, he did. Take a look.'

Four men had just dragged a bear into the clearing.

The ranger went over and peered down at it.

'We're looking for a grizzly,' he said, disgusted. 'Your men shot a black.'

Pat kicked the huge body of the animal. 'He's big enough. How do you know he's not the killer?'

Kelly reached over and drew the Buck hunting knife from the sheath that hung at Pat's belt. He slit the bear's hide up the belly, made a careful incision through the white stomach lining, and reaching in, pawed out a huge handful of half-digested material.

'Grass,' he said. 'Leaves. Maybe a fish. But do you see any human hair? Hair doesn't digest, it matts up into balls.'

'So what?'

'So our bear has eaten the hair off the heads of every one of his victims. There's no hair in this animal's stomach. You just shot down the wrong bear. And as if that weren't bad enough, we're wasting time while the real one is heading somewhere else.'

The radio newsman, reading from his script, continued, 'And the bad news is that there's been another bear killing up in the park today. This time, a ranger. The authorities are now certain they're dealing with a rogue grizzly, and although they're sure of killing or capturing it soon, they want the public to use only the lower camp sites, and even there, to utilize full-sized, hard-top motorhomes or trailers. Avery Kittredge, Park Supervisor, promises a quick return to normal operations, but meanwhile, it has been recommended that not only park visitors, but local residents, stay indoors as much as possible. If you must travel on foot, do so in pairs.'

He made a throat-cutting motion, and the ON THE AIR sign went out.

The reporter turned to his engineer. 'What's the point in traveling in pairs? So the bear can make a sandwich out of you?'

Avery Kittredge's office had been surrounded by the press. A mobile television unit was parked outside the building, with its cables snaking across the sidewalk and a tripod-mounted color camera set up in the lobby.

Inside the supervisor's office, Kelly had just looked up in surprise. He said, 'What did you say?'

'I'm sorry,' Kittredge repeated.

'That helps a lot,' Kelly said. 'Listen, Kittredge, sorry doesn't buy any beans. We've lost a ranger. This has gone far enough. Close the park.'

'Don't push,' said Kittredge. 'I called off the hunters, didn't I? I'll stand aside and let you handle things your way. But we can't close the park. We'd never live it down.'

'I want to call in a company of the National Guard,' said Kelly. 'One from up north. Those boys are all good hunters.'

'And admit things are out of control? Kelly, you've been breathing that thin high country air too long.'

'I've got a plan, damn it. But I need more men.'

'Why?'

Kelly went over to a map of the park which was neatly framed, unlike the one that was simply tacked up on his own office wall. He pointed.

'Look—the first killings took place here.' He indicated the high camp site the two girls had used. 'My guess is, this was the first time he'd tasted human flesh. He liked it. But he couldn't find any more because we chased the back-packers out of the high areas. So he made a circle right about here, and he ended up in one of the lower camp sites, where he ripped open that Dodge pop-top. But he was scared off before he got a chance to eat his victim. So he circled again, and that time he got Gail. Again, he was chased off before he could make a full meal. Then he almost got a hunter, but he had to settle for the baby cub. Finally, he doubled back, moved along our flank, and found Tom. He tore that poor kid up bad, but he still didn't have time to eat before we chased him away.'

'Where does that leave us?'

'I think he's going to keep working his way around in what he considers as his private food larder. A bear's sense of scent is fantastic. He knows where we are. This time, I'd like to get the jump on him. Believe it or not, this bear can think, and he's been one jump ahead of us so far.'

'A bear, even a grizzly, is just an animal, Kelly. Don't invest it with human qualities.'

Kelly said, 'That bear is smarter than you and me put together. Avery, give me a chance. Close the park, and let me call in the Guard.'

'We can't close the park. And asking for outside help—'

'We've got more reporters and TV cameras in there now than we've got rangers. It's turned into a goddamned circus.'

'Cooperate with them,' Kittredge said. 'They're there at my invitation.'

Kelly stared at him. 'You *invited* them?'

'Why not? It won't hurt for the public to know the kind of clean, thorough job we're doing.'

Kelly turned in a full circle, mumbling. When he faced Kittredge again, he said, 'I'm losing my mind. We've got five dead people, and one man in the hospital, and I thought I heard you call that a clean, thorough job.'

'We're doing everything in our power—'

'Balls! You won't give me what I need and—'

'Kelly!' warned the supervisor.

'And now you've called in the media. Kittredge, just now I've figured you out. You don't give a good goddamn whether or not we get that grizzly. What you want is to play Mr. Commander-In-Chief, and get all that juicy press coverage. It might lead to a nice dark brown plastic office in Washington, right?'

'Get out of here,' said Kittredge.

'Well, you just lost your free ride,' Kelly yelled. 'You're not coasting to Washington on *my* back. I've got a responsibility to my men and those people out there, and by God, I'm going to see that it's carried out.'

Coldly, the supervisor said, 'That's it, Kelly. You're finished. Clean out your desk.'

Kelly said, 'Up yours, boss man. That's the nice thing about civil service. You can't fire me. Go on, file your petition. By the time it goes through, I'm going to have that bear.'

He turned and left, deliberately not closing the door.

A reporter popped in and began taking pictures.

A Cinemobile truck had pulled up to the Wildhorse Mountain Lodge, and its crew were busy setting up cameras.

Allison Corwin moved among the throng, taking her own pictures. She was as much interested in those who were there to record the news as the news itself.

A suave reporter, a hand microphone growing from the well-manicured fingers of his fist, stepped up to a middle-aged man near the lodge entrance, glanced over his shoulder to be sure the Eclair NPR 16mm camera was rolling, and said, 'Excuse me, sir. How do you think this bear thing's being handled?'

The man, in a thick southern accent, said, 'Handled? Okay, I reckon. At least they kept the bear away from us folks down here. But I do feel sorry for that Ranger boy.'

The reporter, unctuously, said, 'I'm sure everyone feels the same way.' He turned to a young woman and asked, 'How about you, Miss?'

'Me? What?'

'Apparently there are dangerous bears here in the park. Aren't you afraid to be here with them?'

She looked around. 'I don't see any bears. They don't come around here. I think this thing is getting more publicity than it deserves. If you stay away from trouble, you don't get into trouble, that's my motto.'

At that moment, Kelly pulled up in his Toyota. The reporters swarmed toward him, but he brushed past their questing microphones and went into the lobby. Allison followed him.

He sensed her presence.

When he turned, she smiled and said, 'Click.'

'Click to you,' he replied.

She moved closer, so they couldn't be overheard.

'Kelly . . . I worried about you.'

'No need to.'

She said, 'I'm sorry about Tom.'

'I know.'

'We all liked him.'

'I did too.' He hesitated. 'Allie, I'm sorry about the way I acted. About your book.'

'Not to worry. I got some good photos anyway.'

'You mean you went out there on your own?'

She smiled. 'Never mind. Wait until you see the prints.'

'You're crazy.'

She pinched his rump. 'I know,' she said.

Her father came over. 'How are we doing, Kelly?' he asked.

'Not very well,' said the ranger. He looked around at the crowd thronging the lobby and spilling into the bar. 'What's the matter with these people? Is it morbid curiosity? If it wasn't my job, you couldn't get me within fifty miles of this place.'

Walter Corwin said, 'It's surprising. I didn't expect so many people to stay on. And more keep arriving.'

Allison said, 'It's a big show. They don't feel threatened. Everything around here looks too civilized.'

Kelly said to Corwin, 'Walter, I asked Kittredge to close down the park.'

'And?'

'And he refused.'

'Would it help?'

'I think so.'

'How.'

'If we get rid of all the people, we get rid of that grizzly's source of food. Remember, he's a man-eater now. If he gets hungry, he might go away. Or he might get careless.'

'Then Kittredge was wrong.'

'He usually is.' Kelly paused. 'Walter, how about closing down the lodge?'

Allison said, 'Why? The bear isn't down here.'

'I know. But it's a gesture. A beginning. Here in the lodge, everybody thinks it's safe. If you shut down, you're saying right out in front, it's *not* safe. If you close up, I think I can get the other concessioners to go along. If the private sector takes this seriously, maybe we can force Kittredge's hand, and he'll have to close the park.'

'I can't afford to go it alone,' said Corwin. 'If you can guarantee the others, I'll agree.'

Slowly, Kelly said, 'I haven't spoken with them yet. I had to start somewhere.'

Before Corwin could make an answer, Allison said, 'Kelly, Dad's on the line here. What's happened up in the park is tragic, but he needs this extra business. Things have been tight.'

'Somebody has to be the first to take the plunge. Walter, I need your help.'

'I want to help,' said Corwin. 'But I have stockholders. I have to think of them. Legally, I ought to consult them.'

'There isn't time.'

'You're not being fair, Kelly,' said Allison. 'You're using your friendship with Dad to put him under the gun.'

Kelly realized that he'd lost. He said, 'You're right. Well, it was just an idea. It may not matter much anyway.'

He turned toward the door.

Allison reached for him. He shrugged away her hand.

'Go take your pictures,' he said. And, as he left, he said over his shoulder, 'Click.'

CHAPTER ELEVEN

Kelly's cabin was not much more luxurious than his bare office. The outer walls were of log construction, and the old chinking had begun to fall out so that the cold wind could get its fingers inside when the northers blew.

Kelly stared out the window into the night. The day's hunt had been unsuccessful again.

He sucked on an ice cube from the full glass of scotch in front of him.

Arthur Scott, who was mixing the drinks for the past hour, had made it as light as he dared. Kelly had long since had too much.

Scott renewed the argument.

'How about it?' he asked.

'It's too dangerous,' Kelly said.

'Listen,' said the naturalist, 'your methods have proven themselves to be worthless. Let an expert give it a try.'

'I can't take the responsibility.'

'Your shoulders aren't broad enough to carry it all anyway. Let the rest of us share some of the load.'

'Yeah, Mr. Expert,' Kelly said, the liquor talking. 'What the hell do us civil service rangers know about hunting anyhow? Scott, I used to stalk deer with a home-made bow and arrow, and I always came home with meat.'

'That was a long time ago, Kelly.'

Kelly took a long pull at his drink, too far gone to realize that it was mostly water. 'Yeah, a long time.' He sucked at another ice cube. 'What the hell am I doing in this business anyway? Why didn't I stay in real estate? Do you know how much I could get for this mountain if I could subdivide it and parcel it off?'

Scott said, 'Frankly, I'm not interested in the ravings of a drunk, which is what you are tonight. If you want to hang up your jock strap and get out, go ahead.'

Kelly said, 'Go home, buddy. I'm lousy company, I know it.'

Scott said clearly, 'Kelly, I'm going in after him.'

'You're—'

'Alone. My way.'

'Like hell you are.'

'I have faith in my methods. I can capture him, Kell.'

'Stay out of those woods. That's an order.'

'I can find him. I know the woods better than he does. And when I come up on him, I can put him down.'

'You're crazy, you know that?'

'Maybe,' said the naturalist. 'But I've wasted too much time already. I've got myself a *Ursus Horribulus* to catch.'

The beast hurt.

The bullet wound in his throat ached. The slug had gone through cleanly, without hitting bone or a major artery. But it was a constant reminder to the beast that the two-legged ones had unseen claws that he had not suspected.

Although the bear did not think rationally, he had decided on a primitive level not to give the two-legged ones a chance to hurt him again. He would approach them with stealth and no warning.

Ada Rogers had worked for Walter Corwin for eleven years. Her husband, before he died, had been the general handyman at the lodge, and she had been cooking for its guests since Robert was old enough to walk.

Robert was eleven now, and this early morning before it was time for the school bus, he was playing in the back yard with his pet rabbit.

Ada did not work the breakfast shift, so her time was free until around eleven, when she would begin to prepare for the lunch crowd.

She was sorry for the trouble the bear incidents had brought, but glad, in a bitter-sweet way, because it had resulted in extra business, and Mr. Corwin needed that money. She knew that he had often paid his staff when he really should have laid them off, and that included her.

She called out the window, 'Robert, you stay close to home. The bus'll be along soon.'

He didn't answer. He was trying to get Sam, the rabbit, to eat some carrots. Unlike Bugs Bunny, Sam had absolutely no interest whatsoever in carrots.

His mother shouted again. 'Robert! Do you hear me?'

Reluctantly, he called, 'Yes, Ma.'

'Don't get dirty. You're wearing your good pants.'

'I won't,' he promised.

Sam accepted a slice of carrot. He would really have preferred lettuce, but a captive rabbit eats what he can get.

Behind the trees that fringed the yard, something large moved. Sam saw it, but Robert did not.

Sam the rabbit was no fool. He didn't like the shape of that thing in the trees.

He leaped out of Robert's arms and headed for the fence.

It was of tight-mesh chicken wire, specifically designed to keep Sam from straying. But like all rabbits, Sam had found a soft spot where he could burrow under the wire, and in the past week, he had enlarged the hole in anticipation of just such a moment as this, when he would once again be a free and wild creature.

Sam scooted under the fence.

Then, in the bushes, he stopped.

There was the odor of danger all around him.

Sam began to wonder if it was such a great idea to be free and wild.

Robert had run after him, saw him go under the fence. The boy climbed up the wire and let himself down on the other side. He was trying not to cry. He had kept wild animals before, and he was sure that Sam was gone forever now.

But, to his suprise, Sam was waiting for him under one of the chokeberry shrubs.

Robert caught the rabbit up in his arms and hugged it.

'Don't you run away no more,' he scolded. 'You're a bad bunny.'

He moved back toward the fence.

Behind him, a dark shape followed.

The boy scrambled up over the fence again, holding the rabbit carefully so that it couldn't get away this time.

Inside the house, Ada Rogers went to the television set and switched on the 'Today' program. She liked to listen to Barbara Walters.

Robert stood with his back to the fence, stroking Sam. The rabbit endured it. Stroking meant food was coming soon, and nothing was more important than food.

Behind the boy, the fence was suddenly ripped apart, and the air seemed shattered by a roaring noise. He started to turn, bewildered, and the first thing his eyes caught, high up in the air above him, was the face of a huge bear, the biggest he had ever seen. The black, rubbery nose was thrust forward. The nostrils flared and the mouth, filled with huge white teeth, foamed.

The boy, stunned, was unable to run or to utter a sound.

The rabbit dropped from his numbed hands.

The grizzly came through the fence as if it weren't there, and his huge claws whipped out and raked the boy.

Inside the house, his mother heard the roar of the beast, and the shrill cry that followed. She ran to the window and was horrified by what she saw.

Her child had been hurled against a tree by the huge bear, and his bright blood seemed to be everywhere.

There wasn't a gun anywhere in the house. Ada grabbed the nearest weapon she could find, a poker for the fireplace, and ran out into the back yard.

She screamed as she ran. 'Get away, you! Shoo!'

The bear turned toward her.

When she was close enough, she hit him with the poker.

He dropped the boy and reached for her. She slipped away and hit him again, this time on the snout. He whimpered with pain. For a moment, he seemed ready to turn and retreat.

But he made one more stab at her with his claws, and this time they raked away the front of her dress and half of her breast. She did not feel the pain, and kept flailing at him with the poker, but he knew he had won, and with another lunge, caught her in both paws and drew her close where his huge teeth could finish the job.

Sam, the rabbit, was splashed with some of the blood. His pink tongue licked out, retreated.

He didn't like the taste of this kind of food.

Walter Corwin thought that he might have had a heart attack. He was weak and sweating. He lay on his bed, trembling.

Kelly had asked him to close up. But the money had been more important. Money! It was disgusting.

He'd heard the screams, and ran out in time to fire two shots that drove the huge bear, the biggest goddamned bear anyone had ever seen, away from the bleeding *thing* that had once been Ada Rogers.

And that poor boy. His leg torn off above the knee, his back and chest like mince meat. Corwin's stomach churned just thinking about it now.

Allison had helped him to his room. She wanted to stay with him, but he was ashamed, and wouldn't let her.

He wanted to die himself.

The television people were furious that they weren't allowed to photograph the victims.

Kelly Gordon faced them, like an avenging warrior, and yelled, 'The first bastard who points a camera at those people is going to eat it!'

The ambulance's arrival only increased the agitation of the reporters.

One, holding a cassette recorder, pushed his way up to Kelly and said, 'Who the hell are you to shut us out? The people have a right to know what's going on.'

'They'll know,' Kelly said. 'They'll know the whole damned story. But you're not going to photograph that hurt boy and what's left of his mother. That's final.'

Avery Kittredge arrived. He brushed aside questions by

the reporters and made his way to Kelly, who looked at him coldly.

'Here's the Park Supervisor now,' he said loudly. 'I believe Mr. Kittredge has come to announce that as of this moment, the park is closed. Isn't that so, Mr. Kittredge?'

Trapped, the supervisor nodded. 'In the interests of public safety,' he said. 'Until the situation is under control.'

One reporter said, 'It seems to me this place should have been shut down long before now. You're having a massacre up here.'

'Mister,' said Kelly, 'we're closing our gates to everybody, and that includes the press. So why don't you move along?'

'This isn't park property,' said the reporter.

'No,' said Allison Corwin. 'It belongs to my father. And what Kelly said goes. Move it. All of you.'

'The big carnival's over,' said Kelly. He turned away.

'What about our story?' asked another reporter.

'You'll get it. You'll get one you don't expect. Bears aren't the only dangerous critters in these woods. Stupidity and greed—they're pretty nasty beasts too, aren't they, Kittredge.'

Kittredge ignored him. 'There'll be a press conference in my office at noon,' he told the reporters.

'Don't miss it,' Kelly told them sarcastically. 'After all, you're collaborators in this circus.'

'What are you talking about?' asked one of the newsmen.

'You're as much responsible as that bear up there. You spread the word about all the nice excitement available in the woods for the small price of admission to the park. You made it seem like fun, a chance to find some safe adventure.'

The newsman said, 'We just told it like it was.'

'No,' Kelly said. The ambulance attendants were loading the boy into the back of the vehicle. He nodded toward the small form on the stretcher. 'Only little Robert can tell it like it was. If he lives, maybe he will.'

One of the reporters, looking through field glasses at the ambulance, choked. 'My God,' he said. 'What's that they're putting in there with him?'

Without looking, Kelly said, 'That's Robert's left leg. We got a tourniquet on him in time to save his life. But I wonder if he'll ever feel like thanking us.'

Allison said, 'At least he's still alive.'

Kelly said, 'Part of him is, the poor little son of a bitch.'

CHAPTER TWELVE

Kelly had found the note from Arthur Scott in his office. It read, 'Make sure your boys know what they're shooting at, because I'm going to be up there and I'll probably be wearing my deer skins. When I get him, I'll radio in and let you know where to pick him up.'

Twice, Kelly had Barney try to contact Scott, but the naturalist either wasn't answering, or had his radio turned off.

He left instructions with the duty ranger, 'Keep trying him. Tell him Don and I will be up there in the chopper, and to signal us if we get in his area.'

Although Kittredge had closed the park, he had flatly refused to let Kelly call in the National Guard. However, he had relented to the point of letting Kelly borrow some armament from the local Guard unit, and now Kelly and Don were loading it into the back of the Hughes helicopter.

The biggest piece of gear was a one-man flame thrower. Its tank bore a white star and the stenciled legend, '409th Nat. Guard Batt.'

And there was a grenade launcher, which fitted on the muzzle of a rifle, a box of grenades, and two high-powered rifles. Don asked, 'Which one do you want?'

'Neither. I'll handle the controls. You're a better shot than me.'

Don said, 'You can't keep sliding past it, Kell. It's no different to order a killing than it is to pull the trigger yourself.'

'I know,' Kelly said. 'Where are the flares?'

'In this bag.' Don paused. 'I thought it might happen in Nam, that you'd get yourself backed into a corner where you had to kill or else. But it didn't. You and me, we brought out a lot of bleeding bodies. But you never made any of them bleed. All you did was put your ass on the firing line seven days a week to patch up the damage somebody else had done.'

'You were right there, too.'

'Yeah, but I was shooting back.'

'I remember. Good thing you were, or I might not be here now.'

'Sooner or later, you've got to shoot back, Kell. And I think this is the time.'

'Maybe. Do we have everything?'

Don put two boxes of silvertip expanding bullets in beside the rifles.

'We've got enough to start a war,' he said. 'If we see that bastard, he's dead.'

'But be careful. Scottie's out there somewhere.'

'He's a certified fruitcake,' Don said.

'So you told him.'

'Kell, that goddamned bear'll take that pellet gun of his and chew it up like popcorn.'

'Scott's a good man. He may do what he said he'd do.'

'I hope so. Or we'll be digging another grave.'

Allison drove up. Her smile was wan.

'Kelly . . . you're going up there after him?'

'Yes.'

'I hope you find him.' Her voice trembled. 'I hope you make him suffer before he dies.'

'Allie—'

'I know, he's only a dumb beast. I don't care. He's got it coming.'

'Where's your camera?'

'Packed. Kelly, I'm leaving.'

'What about your book?'

'The hell with my book. If it'd bring back any one of those people, or that boy's leg, I'd throw my camera and every negative I've ever shot right in the middle of Wolf Lake.'

Gently, he said, 'But it wouldn't bring back any of them. You know that.'

Slowly, she nodded. 'Yes, I suppose I do. But I'm sick of

it. I can't commercialize on what's happened here. It'd be like robbing the dead.'

'What will you do?'

'I'm taking Dad back to Ohio, to my aunt's place. He's closed the lodge. He blames himself for the Rogers. He keeps saying that you asked him to close down and he didn't because he wanted the money more than the safety of people.'

'That's nonsense. Nobody's to blame. The bear could just as easily have gone down the other slope, into High City.'

'I know.'

'How is he?'

'All right, but very low. At first we thought it was his heart, but Dr. Hallit says it was just shock and anxiety. But he agrees that it's a good idea to take Dad away from here.'

'Well, tell him I said to get well fast, and maybe we'll have a new rug for his lobby when he opens up again.'

'Don't get hurt trying to collect it,' she said.

'I won't. You take care of Walter.'

'Okay. And you take care of you.'

She started to get in the car, turned. 'You're not off the hook, Kelly,' she said. 'I'm coming back for you.'

'I'll be here,' he said.

She made a little frame with her thumbs and fingers.

'Click,' she said.

There were armed men strung all along the side of the mountain. They were angry, and they were determined.

The beast sensed the danger he was in. He stayed well ahead of the invaders.

And his hunger was growing, without any way to appease it.

Scott had taken Tex, the horse Gail had ridden, and was well up into the high country.

He knew, from occasional monitoring sessions with his radio, that Kelly's rangers were moving along the lower slopes. Where it was safe, they had started controlled fires, to drive the beast into exposed areas where they might get a shot.

Well, he would beat them to it. Because the naturalist was convinced that he knew where the bear would appear next.

Don Stober indicated the thin line of rangers climbing the slope beneath the helicopter.

'There they are,' he said. 'No sign of our bear friend, though.'

'They'll find him. Those boys are good hunters.'

'Some of them. You used to be a hunter. Did you ever ask yourself why you did it?'

'I hunted for meat.'

'Bull. For most hunters, it'd be cheaper to buy their meat from the best restaurant in town instead of spending all the money they do on gear and travel. That's not why they hunt, for the table. That's the justification they give themselves—and their wives. The real reason they hunt is because they're part of a collective unconscious.'

'A what?'

'A drive that's in all of us. You've studied psychology. Some of those eggheads say that we all relate back to our ancestors, the cavemen.'

'And that's why we still hunt?'

'Right. We have this itch to deal with nature on a one to one basis. We're reaching back, trying to be what we once were.'

'Don, you always amaze me. When this is over, I think I'll let you give a few of the women's club lectures.'

'Whoops,' said Don. 'I just lost all interest in psychology.'

'Too late,' Kelly laughed, breaking the tension. 'Your big mouth just got you in a heap of trouble.'

Don banked the chopper.

'See something?' Kelly asked.

'No. It's just a rock.'

'Well, head up toward R-Four,' said Kelly. 'I've got an idea.'

The hunters moved through the forest faster now. The day was warming up, and their jackets were open.

Although they were careful about their targets, shots rang out now and then, booming back and forth between the surrounding hills. Most were fired at shadows, although one round brought down an unlucky black bear who had wandered down below the timber line.

The forest telegraph worked overtime. Beavers slapped their tails on the cold water, warning of danger. Birds chirped and flew, fluttering their wings, to alert the forest's inhabitants that the most dangerous predator of all was approaching.

But, as the long day wore on, the beast stayed well ahead of his pursuers.

The pain in his jaw had begun to bother him again, and the bullet wound in his neck throbbed. He was angry, and frustrated, and above all, he was hungry.

Don had returned to base twice for fuel. Now, near sundown, this was his third run. Once again, Kelly instructed him to head for the high camp area.

'We haven't seen a trace of him up that way,' Don said. 'What makes you think he's going back into the high country?'

'Because he's a bear, and they like to establish a routine. They don't stray from it.'

'This one managed to get all the way down to the lodge. I'd call that straying.'

They flew through a cloud of smoke from one of the deliberately set fires.

Kelly said, 'Yeah, but he ran into lots of trouble. I think Tom hit him. There was hair near the tower. And we've got a small army in the field. He knows it. His logical move is to head for someplace safe, because it's getting too hot and noisy down here.'

As the chopper circled, rising slowly up the elevations of the mountain, Don said, 'And you're going to help him make up his mind.'

'That's what we're doing right now. Showing him that it's going to be mighty uncomfortable if he insists on staying down on the low slopes. He'll get the message.'

The beast ran, moving faster, through the underbrush. Twice some strange object in the sky had passed over him, making fluttering sounds. Both times he had been near cover, and had melted into it, freezing until the creature, whatever it was, had passed over.

The beast was beginning to feel penned in. In every new direction he took, he sensed menace and although he feared no animal in claw-to-claw combat, he dreaded the invisible fang the two-legged ones had that could reach through the air and tear at hair and throat.

Occasionally, he found traces of the markings he had made to identify his range.

Perhaps within that territory things would be better.

Ponderously, he turned uphill.

'There!' Kelly yelled, pointing. 'Right near the camp site.'

He took over the controls as Don grabbed for one of the rifles.

'Hey,' Don said. 'That's not our bear. It's a deer.'

'I know. Drop him.'

Don hesitated. Shooting from a vehicle, even a chopper, is against every sporting rule hunters know. 'It's a doe,' he said.

'Shoot, damn it. We need bait!'

Kelly brought the helicopter in low and smoothly. Don chambered a bullet, brought the crosshairs to bear on the deer's neck, and squeezed off.

She went down, all four legs splayed out, as if a string had suddenly snatched her life away and left only a chunk of flesh bleeding in the forest.

Scott heard the shot, not too far away. But he paid it no mind.

'Damned silly hunters,' he muttered. 'Shooting at their own shadows.'

With the chopper tied down securely in the clearing, in case of a sudden wind, Don and Kelly had made camp near it.

They'd dragged the deer to the edge of the clearing and gutted it out.

'If he's down-wind, he'll smell this,' Kelly said, deliberately puncturing the intestines. The foul odor almost made him choke. But to a grizzly, it was perfume.

They had set up a blind near the chopper, with pine branches piled atop a boulder.

Don scowled at the rifle he held. 'This is a regular army piece,' he said. 'We should have brought something with glass sights you can flip over, to shoot down the barrel in close work.'

'It'll do,' Kelly said. 'Just put the first one between his eyes and you won't have to worry about any close work.'

'I'm not so sure,' Don said. 'That big baby seems to lead a charmed life.'

The beast nosed out the dead deer. But there was another odor mixed with its blood and the ripe scent of its torn intestines. The acrid, disgusting spoor of Man.

The grizzly moved carefully. There was danger here.

But, more importantly, there was food.

The two men talked quietly. They knew that they shouldn't, but the night was dark and lonely.

'What about Allison?' Don asked. 'Are you two serious?'

'I don't know,' Kelly said.

'Well, take it from an expert. *She* is. So if you don't like the game, you'd better get out of it.'

Kelly thought for a moment.

'No,' he said finally. 'I think I like the game.'

'Good. You won't find many better than that girl.'

'What about you?'

Don shrugged. 'I get a little tail here and there. That's all they are to me, nooky. A quick score. I don't hurt anybody. The ones I pick, that's all they're after too.'

'That's pretty temporary, isn't it?'

'Sure. But look who's talking. You've got four years on me, buddy. Wait until I'm your age, maybe I'll think about settling down too.'

'It's a short life,' Kelly said. 'I'm starting to realize that I've wasted most of mine up until now.'

'Different strokes for different folks. You used to be one kind of guy. Now you're becoming another. It happens.'

'Why? Because of one girl?'

'Nope. She just came along at the right time. You're lucky. The two of you are synchronized, just like the blades on that chopper of mine. Do you know what would happen to that bird if those blades came out of sync, and started doing their own thing out of step with each other? It'd tear apart in mid-air.'

Thinking of the night in her cabin, Kelly nodded. 'Yes,' he said. 'I know what you mean.'

'Why don't you take twenty? I'll keep watch. If I get sleepy, I'll wake you.'

'All right,' said Kelly. 'But if you see that son of a bitch, shoot first and wake me later. We've got to put him down.'

Almost gently, Don said, 'We will, Kelly. Don't worry.'

Scott pulled the horse up short. 'Whoa, Tex,' he said. 'I think we've gone far enough for tonight.'

He thought he had been on the trail of the beast, but now he was not so sure.

He picketed the horse near a trickle of water, where there was good grass, and made a wide circle.

Yes, something had moved through here. And it had slept, or at least rested, among the spruces.

He felt the matted pine needles.

They seemed warm.

He went back and unsaddled Tex, then rubbed the horse down carefully.

'You stay right here and eat some of this nice grass,' Scott said. 'I'm going to make myself a bed up there.' He nodded up into the trees. 'But don't you worry, if our friend turns up, I'll keep him away from you.'

Tex whinnied, and began to drink.

Although only a horse, somewhere in his thoughts was a question:

Where was the nice smelling one who used to ride him?

The beast moved cautiously toward the food. He made no sound as he crept through the forest. If he could, he would feed without the two-legged ones even knowing he had been there.

But if he had to, he would challenge them, despite his fear of their invisible fang.

CHAPTER THIRTEEN

Kelly was half-dozing when the bear came.

The beast had approached down wind from the gutted-out deer.

He moved silently, carefully. His feet felt the forest floor and drew back from each dry twig before it had a chance to snap. No Indian could have moved more stealthily.

It was past midnight, and both rangers were dog-tired. Don Stober was sound asleep, breathing noisily through his mouth.

The night was cold, and both men were wrapped in their sleeping bags. The rifle lay against the boulder, with a high-powered flashlight beside it. There was a round in the chamber, but the safety was on.

A pale sliver of a moon hung just above the pine trees. Its light was wan and seemed hardly brighter than that cast by the multitude of stars which twinkled through the dark ceiling of the sky.

On any other occasion, it would have been considered a beautiful night; the kind of night made for love.

But this night, with its chill air and the gentle moan of its wind, had been made for death.

It was the snapping of a bone between mighty jaws that brought Kelly fully awake.

The bear had approached the clearing with care; he knew that the two-legged ones were near, because their scent was almost unbearably strong.

But the beast's hunger made him careless. With his great strength, he might have snatched up the deer carcass and run, to devour it once he had outdistanced the men.

Instead, his mouth drooling with saliva, he could not resist chewing into one of the hindquarters.

The blood was delicious in his mouth, and he bit down too hard, crunching the leg bone.

Kelly sat up with a guilty jerk of his head.

The bear froze. It was very dark. Perhaps the man would not see him.

Carefully, Kelly peered around the boulder. He thought he could see a great dark shape near where they had staked out the deer carcass. He reached over and punched Don in the ribs. Don mumbled something.

Now the dark shape was moving. Kelly aimed the flashlight, and switched it on.

Powered by a six-volt lantern battery, its beam made a golden shaft through the ground mist.

There was definitely something near the deer. Kelly tilted the beam up—higher, and higher, until it seemed he was aiming it directly at the moon itself.

At a point some fifteen feet above the ground, the flashlight found the grizzly's eyes.

They flamed in the darkness like two bright yellow balls. No one who has not caught the eyes of a wild animal in a car headlight or with a flashlight can even begin to imagine the intensity with which they capture, amplify, and reflect illumination.

It's a frightening sensation, when you are alone in the woods at night, to suddenly see two terribly brilliant orbs staring back at you from the darkness. And the reflection has an eerie quality of being *transparent*, as if you were looking through the amber eyes into another world.

Kelly almost gasped. He could not see any details of the bear's body or head, but the eyes, so high above the ground, were terrifying in themselves.

He punched Don again and whispered, 'Hey. He's here.'

Don mumbled, 'Wha— ?' and came awake.

His voice galvanized the grizzly into motion. The eyes vanished from Kelly's flashlight, and the two rangers heard the crashing of frenzied flight through the trees.

They leaped up. Don grabbed the rifle; Kelly took a bag

of grenades, and the flashlight. They ran toward the deer carcass.

Kelly pointed, with the flashlight beam, at a torn patch of underbrush.

'He went that way,' he said. 'I'll lead. You follow with the rifle. But be careful which one of us you shoot!'

Almost at a full trot, they followed the bear's trail, which looked as if a bulldozer had rooted a path through the woods.

The grizzly was angry. This was not the first time today food had been literally snatched from his mouth. Without making it a conscious thought, he considered ambushing the two who were following him.

The plan was discarded immediately.

He feared that invisible fang.

But there was another way.

He increased his speed, and slowly, began to make a giant circle.

The two rangers were out of breath. Running uphill through a dense forest is not easy, even for a man in good shape.

They had lost the grizzly's trail and could not find it again. Angling back and forth along the mountainside, they hoped to cut it, but after fifteen minutes of fruitless searching, they abandoned the effort.

'You *had* him,' Don said, disbelievingly. 'You had the son of a bitch froze dead still in your light. And you didn't shoot. Why the hell not?'

'I thought you would.'

Don cursed. 'Well, we've lost him now.'

'We were right behind him. How can he move without leaving a trace?'

'There's traces, only we'll never find them at night. He's long gone until daylight.' Don coughed. 'I ain't the man I used to be. We must have run a mile straight up the side of this lousy mountain.'

'We might as well head back to camp and get some sleep,'

Kelly said. 'We'll need to be as sharp as we can be in the morning.'

'Kell . . .'

'I know. You don't have to say it. If I'd pulled that trigger, we wouldn't have to worry about tomorrow morning. I think when this is over, I'm going to pack it in, Don. A ranger who can't shoot when he has to isn't worth very much.'

They descended in silence.

The deer carcass was gone.

Don Stober looked down at the bloody spot where it had been and unleashed a string of oaths that nearly turned the air blue.

'He doubled back,' Kelly said, half in admiration. 'The bastard lured us up the mountain, circled back, and went home with his breakfast.'

Don said, 'I used to believe that animals couldn't think, at least not like folks do. But this baby's been ahead of us every step of the way. I do believe the rascal's playing with us like we were toys.'

'Maybe we are,' Kelly said glumly. He examined the rest of the camp to see if anything else had been taken or damaged. But the grizzly had been satisfied with the deer meat.

Don peered into the darkness. 'Maybe he's around here close, waiting for us.'

Kelly said, 'I think he went off somewhere to eat in peace.'

'And once he's finished, what's to stop him from circling back again looking for a dessert course? I tell you, old buddy, this boy is scared.'

'Me too,' said Kelly. 'Keep that rifle handy.'

As Kelly dragged out his sleeping bag, Don said, 'All right, but I think instead of snoring this time, I'm going to do me a heap of concentrated *listening*.'

He spread out his own sleeping bag, crawled into it without taking off any of his clothing or even his shoes. The rifle was on the ground within easy reach.

The moon was higher now, and silvery white clouds scudded across its face.

'Good-night,' Kelly said.

'Nighty-night,' said Don. 'Later on, if you feel a wet snout on your face, it isn't me. Whatever you do, don't move, and especially don't kiss it back.'

'Very funny,' said Kelly, chuckling. At least Don was back to his usual good spirits.

Distantly, a wolf or wild dog howled.

'I feel the same way, good buddy,' said Don Stober.

The wind moaned and more clouds invaded the star-speckled sky, and soon the two tired rangers were asleep.

Scott was moving before the sun came up. During the long night, he had slept only fitfully. Once he had been awakened by the crashing of some large animal through the brush, and before dozing off again had taken careful note of its location. That would be the first area he investigated when daylight came.

His breakfast was a double handful of raisins and dried fruit. Today's ranger carried compressed ration bars, or instant breakfasts marketed for the harried commuter. They were convenient and good, but Scott still preferred the old ways.

As a treat for Tex, he had brought along a small package of sugar cubes.

Now he held out two, and the horse lipped them off the palm of his hand. Tex nibbled on them while Scott saddled him up.

'Those boy scout rangers,' Scott said, adjusting the cinch, 'what do they know? Biggest mistake they ever made was in cutting down on horseback patrols, started using those four-wheel drives. You can't talk to a jeep; can't scratch its ears, either.' He gave Tex a few gentle scratches, and the horse made a snorting sound of pleasure. 'Sure as hell can't feed it a lump of sugar.'

He tied his blanket roll on behind the saddle, and took

one last walk around the rough camp area to make sure he hadn't left anything.

To the horse, he said, 'Okay, looks like we've got everything we came in with. Let's hit the trail, partner.'

He swung himself up into the saddle, and guided Tex over the mountainside toward where he had heard the noise last night.

The grizzly had eaten perhaps half of the hundred-and-sixty-pound deer, and had buried the rest for later use.

The carcass was not totally buried, for the bear had merely scooped out a shallow pit with its claws, and tumbled mixed earth and leaves over the grave.

In two or three days, longer in cold weather, the meat would reach that ripe state of decay that appeals so strongly to a bear's appetite. If the blow flies got to it, and the carcass became maggot-infested, so much the better.

The bear was thirsty now, and he had a craving for something acid—perhaps late berries, if he could find some by the stream, or an entire village of ants dug out of their hill.

His keen nose told him that the nearest water was over the next ridge.

The grizzly set out toward it.

It had been a long time since he'd wanted fish. But now he did.

Scott studied the sign.

Something had come through here in a big hurry.

It might have been a bear . . . or maybe a stray moose. It was hard to tell. The ground was so hard and rocky, whatever tracks there were had not left clear markings.

His hand touched his radio.

No. He did not want to mislead the searchers. If they came up here and found only a moose in early rut, the real quarry might be escaping through the area they'd left unprotected.

Whatever it had been, it had followed a natural trail

which was grown up with disuse. Branches were broken, or twisted, along its path.

There was plenty of clearance for him and the horse. Slowly, alert to any movement, he traced the animal's marks of passage.

The sun was up now, and felt warm on his face. He cocked his head and listened. Around him, the forest was still—but somewhere ahead, and not too far away, birds cried a warning. Was it because of the approach of man and horse . . . or for some other intruder?

He checked his holster to be sure the tranquilizer gun was there.

Tex made a snorting sound.

Scott patted his neck. 'Easy,' he said. 'I know. You smell something you don't like. It's all right, boy. We're looking for him.'

The tone of his voice soothed the horse.

Warily, he urged Tex forward.

Now the birds fell quiet altogether.

The horse shied, and almost threw him. Scott tightened the reins, squeezed his knees to maintain balance.

Something had torn up the earth here in the center of a small clearing. It looked like a rough grave.

He dismounted and went over.

Blood seeped through the earth and leaves. He scraped away at the mound, and saw the mutilated head of a doe deer.

She had been half-eaten. Both ears were gone, and the white of the skull showed through the mangled flesh in several places.

Scott nodded. Half to himself, half to the horse, he said, 'We've got him, Tex.'

The horse, nervous, pawed the ground. Only years of training kept him from tossing the reins and fleeing down the mountain. But the man's presence, and his calm voice, held the animal in place.

Scott said, into his radio, 'Hey, Kelly, how about it? Do you copy?'

He had to call twice more before receiving an answer.

'Scottie! Where are you?'

'Up by December Gap. On the west slope. I think I'm on our friend's trail.'

'Are you sure? We're over in the Spring Meadow area, and we know for sure he was here last night. We baited him out with a deer carcass and damned if he didn't steal it right from under our noses.'

Scott chuckled. 'Well, look no further. He buried what's left of it right here.'

Kelly said, 'Can we get the chopper in there?'

Scott looked around. 'That's a negative. Too many trees. There's a clearing maybe half a mile down the slope that might work.'

'You stay put until we get there,' Kelly ordered. 'Don't start any arguments with that grizzly. I saw him last night. He's big, and he's mean.'

'Ten-four,' said Scott.

He switched off the radio and replaced it in his belt holster. To Tex, he said, 'Ten-four means okay in radio talk, Tex. And in my talk, it also means a lie. If I wait for them to get up here, he's going to get clean away—either that or they'll spot him from the chopper and shoot him dead.'

He checked the tranquilizer gun to be sure it was loaded. The big shell with its glass pellet was chambered.

Scott took a rope from his saddle bag and, with distaste, knotted it around the remains of the deer. He threw a half hitch over his saddle horn, patted Tex on the flank. 'Hup, boy. Pull him out of there.'

The horse backed up and the deer carcass slid out of the shallow grave. The left rear leg was gone, and the abdomen had been savaged until the animal was almost cut in two there. The horse whinnied and tried to get away from the bloody thing. Scott caught the reins.

'Ho, ho,' he soothed. 'It's all right, boy.'

Tex gentled somewhat, but the sharp smell of blood kept his ears flicking nervously.

Carefully, Scott mounted. 'We're going to drag this carcass and leave a blood trail,' he said. 'Mr. Bear'll come back and find his lunch missing, and my guess is he'll take out after it. We'll be waiting. There's a good perch a quarter of a mile up the mountain that'll give me a better shot at him than I could get here.'

The horse pranced and tried to get further away from the dead thing on the ground. But now he was tied to it.

Some think that animals have premonitions of danger and doom. An example is the howling dog outside a death watch.

No one has ever attributed such foreshadows to man's servant, the horse, however.

But at that moment, Tex seemed to feel a cold wind, coming down the mountain and chilling him worse than the coldest winter he had ever endured.

Kelly radioed the grizzly's new location down to the men at the ranger station, and to those who had camped out on the mountain.

'Get some troops around by the big rock slide,' he ordered. 'If he gets past us, and the rangers on the slope, he might come down that way. Don't take chances.'

'That's what you should have told Scottie,' Don grumbled.

'I told him to stay put,' Kelly said, loading the rest of the gear into the chopper. 'He said he would.'

'I heard,' said Don. 'The difference is, you believed him. I didn't. That man's crazy. I'll give you five to one he's on that bastard's trail right now with his little pop gun and a glass bullet.'

He would have lost. Scott wasn't on the grizzly's trail.

The grizzly was on *his*.

Scott's plan would have worked if he had taken just two minutes more lead time over the grizzly. The protective ledge where he planned to wait in ambush was actually in sight up the slope.

The attack came without warning, and was horrifyingly effective.

The beast appeared suddenly just feet away, rising up out of the small trees and underbrush like a giant mass of golden hair, shot through with white and dark. He towered over the horse and rider and his jaws gaped wide, all white teeth and flowing saliva. His roar was a fearful obbligato to the frightened cry of the horse, whose feet pawed at the rocky hill and slipped as the animal tried to leap into flight.

Scott had almost no time to react, but his hand dipped for the tranquilizer gun. There was no time to draw the rifle from its scabbard on the right side of the saddle.

The grizzly flicked out his great paw, studded with six-inch claws, and before the naturalist's horrified eyes, *ripped* the screaming horse's head away from the mount's neck.

Reflexively, Tex shied away from the blow and as Scott tried to scramble from the saddle, the headless horse, amazingly, took two long strides up the trail, pumping blood from the torn neck arteries in hose-like streams.

Scott, riding the headless apparition, found his voice and shouted, 'God damn you!' at the grizzly.

Then the dead horse faltered and, in slow motion, fell.

Scott was pinned under the twitching body.

The bear came toward him.

He tried to get at the rifle again. But it was out of reach under the dead horse.

The grizzly roared again. Cold fear gripped the naturalist. Inside his head, a voice cried, *Not me! Not now! I'm not ready!*

He had seen many living things die. He had even been able to accept the abstract idea of his own death.

But now that it was upon him, he would not admit it into his presence.

Part of him wanted to plead for mercy, to beg God to save him. Another part fought back.

That part managed to free the tranquilizer pistol which was jammed between his crushed hip and the rocky mountainside. He cocked the hammer, lifted it, and aimed directly into the grizzly's open mouth,

Gone were all thoughts of capturing the beast, of studying it, of its value to science.

I want to live, his mind shrilled.

He squeezed the trigger, and the charge exploded in the oddly shaped gun.

It was in that moment that his luck ran out.

Scott had been in tight spots before. But somehow he had always found that unexpected handhold on the cliff, that extra gasp of breath in the pounding surf, that lucky ricochet of bullet that stopped a charging water buffalo in Uganda.

This morning all the luck was gone.

A chance wind blew a small branch between him and the grizzly, the glass bullet struck it, and exploded in the air. The chemicals that were supposed to paralyze the bear scattered themselves over the swaying needles of the tree.

There was no time to reload. The enraged grizzly literally tore the horse's body away from him and hurled it against a rock. The body struck with a horrid belch of air being expelled from the dead lungs.

Scott managed to roll away from the beast's first charge. He caught up a deadfall branch. It was a poor weapon, but all he had. His leg hurt terribly. It kept him from even considering trying to outrun the monster.

He hoped that the beast would turn to the dead horse. It was food ready for the eating.

But red anger had taken control of the grizzly. He had been on the run from the two-legged ones as long as he could remember.

He advanced toward the naturalist.

Scott waited for his chance, then jabbed the fallen branch directly into the bear's eye.

The grizzly screamed with rage and pain, and Scott slipped around the edge of a rock ledge. If he could roll down the hill and get into one of the small caves. . . .

'He doesn't answer,' Kelly said, pressing the radio beeper alert again. His open voice transmissions hadn't raised Scott, so maybe this would signal the naturalist that he was being called.

'I told you,' Don said. 'He's tracking that goddamned bear. Pay up.'

'Let's get this chopper moving,' Kelly said, strapping himself in. 'I've got a bad feeling.'

Scott might have been safe, because the bear, in pain, had drawn back, and now that the agony in his eye was subsiding, had begun to move toward the bleeding body of the horse.

Then the radio in the man's belt holster made a BEEP! that drew the grizzly's attention to him again.

Hopelessly, Scott began to run. But the bear was upon him in two strides, and the great talons ripped his windbreaker and his shirt, and half of his *chest* away, as Scott stared in shocked disbelief.

He fell to his knees and tried to stop the blood with both hands.

The huge claws tore a huge chunk from his back and shoulders.

Slowly, the man collapsed face down into his own blood.

The helicopter made a circle over the December Gap area.

'Nothing,' said Don Stober. 'Not a thing on the move.'

'He's down there somewhere.'

'Unless he got his position mixed up.'

'Not Scottie. Make another pass.'

'You're the boss. But if there's anything down there, we ought to have seen it. Scott's on horseback, isn't he? How the hell could we miss a horse?'

'How could we miss a fifteen-foot grizzly? But we have.'

'One more pass coming up,' said Don.

He tilted the chopper over so steeply that Kelly could look straight down through his side window at the spiked tops of the pines, pointing up at the rangers like so many green fingers.

Consciousness returned slowly.

Pain throbbed through every nerve of Scott's body. It was the pain he became aware of first. Then, as if from a long distance, an impression of light—and then its actual presence—moved toward him.

He opened his eyes.

The bear was feeding on what was left of the horse.

Scott lay absolutely still. Something had awakened him from that sleep so close to death.

He heard it again.

The flopping whirling of a helicopter's blades.

It seemed to come closer. But then it faded.

They were looking for him.

Scott felt a faint trace of hope stir within him. If he played dead, the bear might be satisfied with the horse meat.

His eyes were slits. He could see the bear from the corner of his field of vision. The sounds that it made, crunching the flesh and bones of Tex, were sickening. Added to his own pain and fear, it was almost enough to make Scott vomit. But he choked down the mucus and bile. He must not make noise. That would be sure death.

He let his body flatten against the earth.

What a waste. A creature like that, driven to murder by whatever unknown compulsions. Any naturalist worthy of the name would travel halfway around the world to see a throwback such as this.

But there was no hope for the grizzly, and little enough for he himself. He did not know how extensive his wounds were, but they were serious. He sensed the loss of blood in the waves of dizziness that swept over him every time he moved his eyes, however slightly.

He must have fainted, then, because the next thing he was aware of was the sound of digging.

The bear was clawing a shallow trench in the ground just feet away from the man.

My God, Scott thought, he's going to bury me!

Then he realized that was good, that it was his only hope. He could lie there, playing dead, until the bear wandered off. Then maybe he could get away, or raise help with the radio.

The digging noises stopped.

Scott felt his insides seem to shrivel up.

The bear was coming to get him.

CHAPTER FOURTEEN

With the number of men in the woods, it was a miracle that no one was seriously hurt. There were several near misses, as nervous rangers shot at what they thought was the grizzly. But no one was even wounded. Several falls resulted in minor injuries, and one ranger got lost and wandered in circles until he dropped from exhaustion only a few hundred feet from the base camp he'd started from.

Don Stober had circled the December Gap area three times, without seeing anything worth going down for a closer look. He returned to base for fuel, and while they were taking it on, Avery Kittredge arrived.

'It's obvious that you're incapable of handling this affair,' he told Kelly. 'I've decided to ask for help from the National Guard. When their commander arrives, give him whatever cooperation he requests.'

Kelly almost hit the supervisor. 'You headline-grabbing bastard,' he said. 'I wanted the Guard in here two days ago. If we'd had them, Tom Cooper would probably be alive right now. Well, we can use the manpower. But if their commander wants me, he'll have to come up on the mountain, because that's where I'm going to be. Scottie's spotted our bear. He needs help, and right now, not tomorrow.'

'My instructions,' began the supervisor. He shut his mouth when Don Stober waved at him.

Don said, 'Mr. Supervisor, if I were you, I'd close my trap before either the flies or Kelly's fist settle in it. Just a little friendly advice.'

'Let's go,' said Kelly, crawling into the helicopter.

They took off in a whirling blast of rotor backwash, blowing Kittredge's hat down the hill.

'He's going to get you fired,' Don said. 'Probably me too.'

'Let him,' Kelly said. 'Who the hell cares? Let's go get our bear before Scottie makes a house pet out of him.'

The grizzly was far from being a pet.

He studied Scott carefully. The two-legged one seemed dead, he had not moved, and the smell of blood was everywhere on him.

Yet the bear hesitated. He did not understand wounding further merely to be sure his prey was dead. If it looked and smelled dead, it *was* dead.

He had eaten well of the dead horse. Its blood and the torn shreds of its flesh were smeared all over his great snout. His belly was distended, bloated.

This meat could be buried for a while, and he would eat it when it ripened.

The grizzly reached down and scooped up Arthur Scott, like a housewife at the market scoops up a handful of loose string beans.

Scott felt one of the claws go through his chest, into his lung. He bit his lip to keep from crying out. If he made a noise, he would be torn to bits.

A hazy darkness began to descend over him. He fought it away.

Even if he had a punctured lung, many men had lived through that. He must not move, he must not even seem to breathe.

He felt himself being thrown into the shallow pit, and then he almost choked as fresh dirt and damp leaves were thrown into his face. But he managed to control the spasm.

He felt his blood leaking out into the ground. Slowly, he managed to slip his hand around to cover the wound. With luck, the blood would clot. But the claw had left a sucking hole there, and his breath moved in and out through it.

Scott knew he had only hours to live, if he didn't get help.

He waited.

The bear went back for another snack from the entrails of the mangled horse. Scott heard the crunching and the slurping as the beast ate. He willed himself into immobility, into death-like silence.

If ever a man had earned his life through sheer courage and determination, it was Arthur Scott in those long moments as he lay buried in his own grave.

Kelly's radio beeped.

He hit the button. 'Kelly.'

They were orbiting the high country, looking for anything, any clue.

The voice that came was weak. 'Scott . . . hurt . . .'

'Scottie! Where are you?'

'December Gap. Half-buried. Bear killed . . . horse. Mauled me.'

'We're on our way,' Kelly rasped. 'Hang in there.'

'He's gone . . . I've got to get out of this hole, hide someplace. Come quick . . . bleeding . . .'

'Five minutes,' Kelly promised. Don had put the chopper into a screaming dive, heading down the mountain toward December Gap.

'Locking transmitter button on . . .' gasped the naturalist. 'No strength . . . look for me in . . . trees.'

They could hear the grating sound of the earth, as he pawed it away, the gasping and whistling of his breath.

He choked, 'I'm out. I'm—'

There was a pause.

Then something growled.

Scott's voice said, 'Oh, my God, no.'

And, because the naturalist's transmitter was locked in the on position, for the next thirty seconds they listened while Arthur Scott died.

They had run up the hill, although they knew they were far too late. Looking down at Scott, they gasped for breath. They had not remembered to bring a ground cloth or blanket.

Kelly took off his parka and draped it over what remained of Scott's face.

'What now?' Don asked dully. 'Do we take him down?'

'No time,' Kelly said. 'That thing's getting away.'

'We can't leave him here like this—'

'Let's move.'

'But there's other wild life up here. They'll—'

'Let them. It's too late for Scottie. But it's not too late for us to get that bastard. He can't be too far away.'

As they half ran, half staggered, down to the landing site, Don said, 'Kelly, believe me, I truly never meant that feller any harm.'

'I know it,' Kelly said. 'Run.'

They got the chopper off the ground in record time.

'Take her right over Scottie,' Kelly said. 'That's our starting point.'

'Okay. Hang on.'

They scraped the tree tops, and buzzed the little clearing with its two terribly still chunks of bleeding meat that had been, only an hour before, a man and a horse.

'Take us uphill,' said Kelly.

'How do you know?'

'I don't know. But that's where he's going. That bastard's headed back where it all started, up to R-Four.'

'Why? There's nothing there now.'

'*He* doesn't know that. Damn it, Don, pour on the coal. Let's spot him before he gets under cover.'

He fumbled in the storage area behind the seat and came up with a bag of grenades.

'What do you figure on doing?'

Kelly said grimly, 'Blowing his lousy hide into ribbons.'

Don gave a low whistle. 'So it's finally pushed you to where you'll shoot back.'

'And then some,' Kelly said. He laid three of the grenades out near his foot. He unlatched the hatch and slid it back, locked it there. Now it was as if he were flying through the air with nothing between him and the blurred landscape below but a tiny strip of metal.

Don asked, 'Why R-Four?'

'Why does a salmon kill himself to swim back to the little hollow in the stream where he was spawned? Something programs them, like a computer. And this grizzly's programmed, too.'

Softly, Don said, 'Just like us.'

'There!' Kelly said, pointing.

They saw the trees parting beneath them and ahead a few hundred feet. Something monstrously large was plunging through them, heading up the mountain.

'Son of a bitch,' said Don, glimpsing the grizzly. 'He's one hell of a bear.'

'Swing in over him,' Kelly said, pulling the pin from one of the grenades. He held the firing lever tightly and leaned halfway out the open hatch.

The beast knew fear, genuine fear, for the first time in his life.

Above him, the strange bird circled. It was obviously pursuing him.

He twisted and turned, but he could not outrun it, and he could find no place to go to earth, to hide.

Something fell from the bird. It hit a few yards down the mountainside, and then there came a great noise and a huge paw tore at his fur and hurled him to one side. He fell against a spruce, almost knocking it down, and then lurched on his headlong flight again.

The grizzly had been peppered with metal fragments and chips of exploded rock, but they did not penetrate his thick hide, and only the concussion had been noticed.

He came to a stream and splashed through it, throwing water in a plume ten yards high.

Another object fell, and this time the hammer of its blast *hurt* the beast. He fell to one side, clawing at a patch of blood that had appeared on his leg, and chewed at the wound until he realized that the thing in the sky was approaching again.

He reared to his full height and reached for it, but it was too high, and he fell down to all fours and began the furious plunge up the mountain once more.

'Take her down closer,' Kelly said. 'I almost got him that time.'

'Let me hover, get him with the rifle. I don't want to get any closer to those trees, Kell.'

'No time. He'll be over the mountain and gone.'

'So? Isn't that what we want?'

Kelly said, his voice dead, 'No. We want him stretched out cold.'

Don tilted the chopper down, but he didn't descend fast enough to suit Kelly, who put on a little more forward pressure on his own control yoke.

'Hey!' Don yelled.

'He's coming up on the clearing,' Kelly shouted. 'Keep on top of him.'

He pulled the pin of the third grenade.

'Don't drop that thing in here with us!' Don warned.

Kelly heaved it out the hatch. This time, the giant grizzly was hurled almost headlong out into the clearing where the two girls had camped that first day.

'Got the bastard!' Kelly shouted. He turned to reach for the rifle, and Don misunderstood, thought Kelly had the controls, and reached for his own weapon.

Unpiloted for a fraction of a moment, the chopper tilted and one blade tipped a tree.

Don grabbed for the yoke. 'Holy Christ,' he said 'I thought you had it.'

'Bad?'

'Tip's gone from one rotor blade. I've got to take her down, or we'll come apart.'

He feathered the blades and slipped the Hughes down into the clearing. For a moment they both lost sight of the grizzly, but the bear never took his eyes off them, and when the strange bird settled down, he was rushing toward it, and caught it in midair and threw it savagely to the ground.

He had never touched metal before, and when he tried to claw and bite the ugly thing from the sky, his teeth closed around cold, tasteless hardness.

Don was thrown from the chopper, carrying with him the army rifle. He landed heavily near the edge of the clearing.

Kelly, pinned in the wreckage, fumbled at his harness. Don's had broken cleanly at one of the attach points.

The grizzly, ignoring the fallen man on the ground, reached toward Kelly. He had never seen transparent plastic, either, and it foiled him for a few seconds. His claws made white tearing marks on its surface.

Don, dizzy from the fall, lifted his rifle and fired into the animal's shoulder. The heavy slug made a meaty slap as it exploded against the grizzly's muscles, and the impact staggered the bear.

He looked around, seeking the source of this new pain.

Don fired again. The second bullet shattered one of the bear's ribs. But his huge body soaked up the two-thousand-pound-plus impact of the slug.

This one had the invisible fang! With a roar, the grizzly hurled himself across the dozen yards separating him from the fallen man.

Don had time to fire once more, but this bullet missed completely. And then the grizzly had him around the upper torso, the razor claws ripping through his flight suit and his flesh.

Staring death in the face, Don let out a cry of rage. He grabbed for his sheath knife, began to slash the bear across the shiny black snout.

Now it was the bear's turn to roar with anger. His great jaws opened, moved toward the ranger's unprotected throat.

His head jerked with a sudden impact.

Kelly had managed to half-free himself from the twisted wreckage, and had glanced a thirty-ought-six bullet off the beast's skull.

Another slug mangled his ear.

Dropping the forgotten ranger, the beast turned back toward the helicopter.

Kelly emptied the five-shot magazine into him. Every bullet hit him home, tearing gobs of hair and bloody flesh away with each impact. But the bear kept coming.

Kelly threw the empty rifle aside and his grasping hand found the last of the grenades. He pulled the pin and threw it.

He overthrew. It exploded behind the grizzly, and its concussion only pushed the beast toward the wrecked chopper even faster.

Kelly tried to free himself from the wreckage, but couldn't. He felt in the storage area for anything else to use as a weapon.

His fingers closed on the tank of the flame thrower. He pulled at it, but it was jammed.

He twisted around, got both hands under the crumpled metal of the chopper's seat, and heaved. He felt pain shoot through all the way to the bone, but he kept pulling.

Suddenly, the tank came free, and with it, the nozzle and firing unit.

The bear was reaching into the flight compartment when he managed to fire the automatic striker, and the manifold began to glow.

Still, he would have been too late except for the shot that Don fired just then, staggering the grizzly slightly and slowing his attack.

The bear was actually dead at that moment. He had absorbed enough lead to kill two or three his size. But his instincts still ruled, and they ordered him to destroy his attackers.

He reached for Kelly with the terrible claws.

The nozzle almost in the grizzly's face, Kelly pressed the ejection lever and a stream of flaming napalm-like burning oil covered the bear. Instantly, the air fumed with the smell of burning hair.

The grizzly gave a horrible roar and leaped backward, pawing at the flames with both front feet. But after one snort of agony, when he inhaled the searing flames into his lungs, he contorted into a pain-whipped bundle of burning flesh and hair that writhed on the ground and died as slowly and painfully as any death can be.

Kelly was sickened by it. He lowered his head and choked.

He felt the hatch on his side of the chopper tremble. Don, bleeding and torn, but alive, had crawled there.

'I hear the troops coming up the hill,' he said. 'Late but welcome.'

'You all right?'

'No, but I think I'll live. Thanks to you. How about yourself?'

'I don't think I'll ever be all right again,' Kelly said.

Don reached up and gripped his arm. 'Yes you will. People are tough. You'll see.'

Kelly didn't answer.

He stared at the beast that had come over the mountain, now just a flaming lump of charred meat and hair, and there were tears in his eyes.

EPILOGUE

The last thing the beast knew, before darkness closed in forever, was the hated stench of man and of burning oil.

GWEN IN GREEN

HUGH ZACHARY

Gwen and George seemed like any other young couple planning their ideal home. After several years of marriage his parents' death in an aircrash had suddenly made them rich – and able to build the house they had always dreamed about.

The house was beautiful, isolated on its island and ringed with forest. And at first only the distant sound of the bulldozers clearing the forest disturbed their peace. But suddenly Gwen, who all her life had been paralysed by a sense of shame, discovered a new sensuality lurking in her unsuspecting body. And soon even George's loving attention was not enough. For as the bulldozers tore into the forest near the house Gwen felt the plants' pain rending her own flesh. And there was only one way to drown the pain . . .

CORONET BOOKS

NESSIE: Seven Years in Search of the Monster

FRANK SEARLE

DOES NESSIE REALLY EXIST?

Myth? Or Monster?

In his tent on the banks of Loch Ness, Frank Searle is the man with the answers.

On 16th June 1969 Frank Searle pitched his tent on the south bank of Loch Ness. Since then he has put in more than twenty thousand hours systematically watching the Loch. In this time he has been rewarded with more sightings of its strange prehistoric inhabitants than almost any other individual, and with some of the most amazing photographs ever taken. Here, with those photographs, is the story of Loch Ness and one man's search for the truth.

CORONET BOOKS